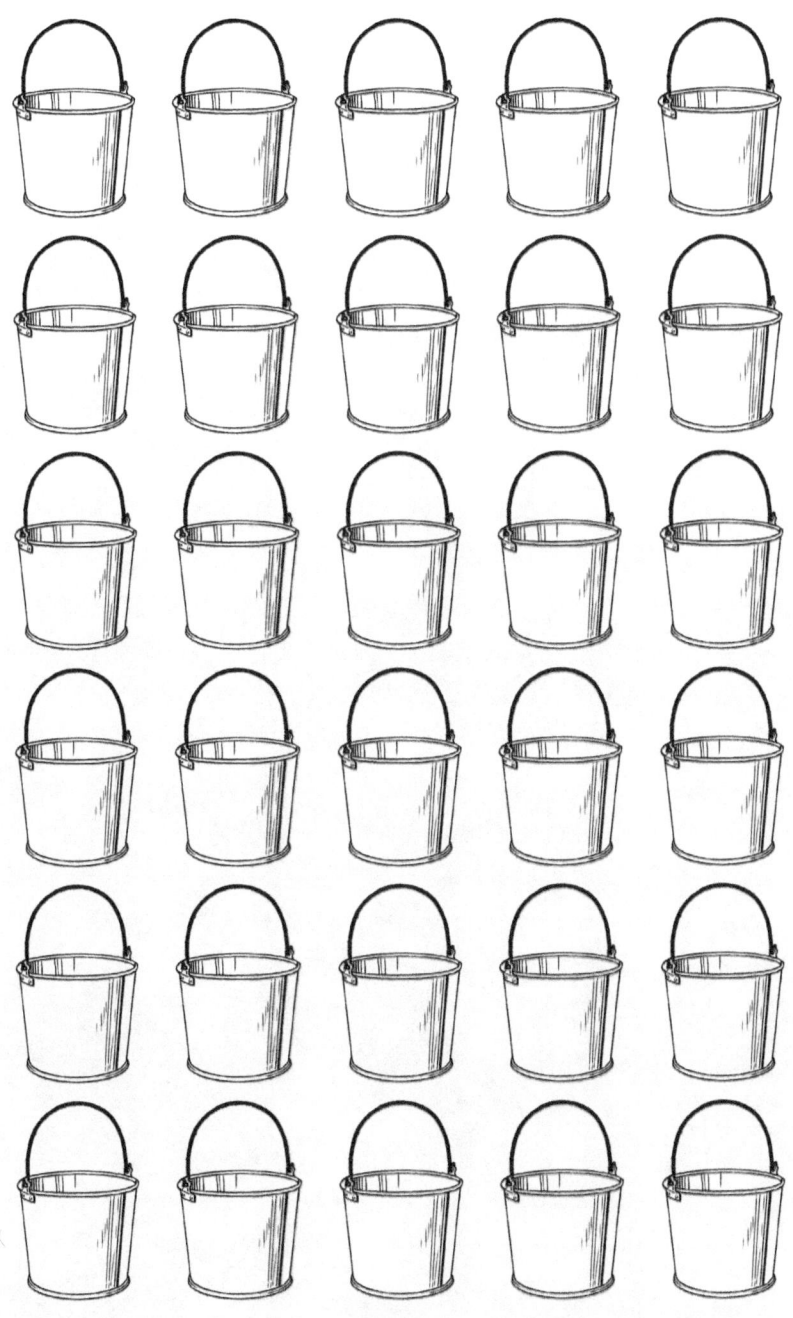

Pure Slush Books

2014

February

Vol. 2

a Pure Slush book

Pure
Slush

2014 February Vol. 2 is edited by Matt Potter and
published by Pure Slush, December 2013.

All stories are copyright © of the individual authors

Cover photographs copyright © Alicia Solario

ISBN: 978–1–925101–14–0

You can find *Pure Slush* at http://pureslush.webs.com

Copies of all *Pure Slush* publications can be bought
at http://pureslush.webs.com/store.htm

All queries re *Pure Slush* can be made
via email to edpureslush@live.com.au

A note on differences in punctuation and spelling

Pure Slush proudly features (both online and in print) writers from all over the English–speaking world. Some speak and write English as their first language, while for others, it's their second or third or even fourth language. Naturally, across all versions of English, there are differences in punctuation and spelling, and even in meaning. These differences are reflected in the stories *Pure Slush* publishes, and it accounts for any differences in punctuation, spelling and meaning found within these pages.

stories by

Guilie Castillo–Oriard

Townsend Walker

Derek Osborne

Gloria Garfunkel

John Wentworth Chapin

Lynn Beighley

Andrew Stancek

Rachel Ambrose

Gill Hoffs

Susan Tepper

Jessica McHugh

Shane Simmons

Michelle Elvy

Len Kuntz

Michael Webb

James Claffey

Gwendolyn Joyce Mintz

Stephen V. Ramey

Gay Degani

Sally–Anne Macomber

Mandy Nicol

Margaret Bingel

Darryl Price

Teresa Burns Gunther

Matt Potter

Gary Percesepe

Nathaniel Tower

Kimberlee Smith

for

Theo,

Mr Boom Boom,

such a handsome boy

M.P.

Saturday, 1ˢᵗ February 2014

The Chablis and Sushi Miracle

by Guilie Castillo−Oriard

Just past ten AM Luis Villalobos walks into the lobby of Ehrlich
Fiduciary with a thick binder in one hand and a hazelnut
cappuccino in the other. He's already a regular at the Barista
place, even though it means a detour. Given this island's
appalling lack of choice, good cappuccino − strong, the foam
thick enough to chew − is worth any sacrifice. Mornings like
today it might warrant arson. Or murder.

In the elevator he takes a grateful sip and squares his
shoulders for the mirror. He didn't shave, and his hair is still wet
from the shower. At least it's gelled and combed. His shirt is
untucked, sleeves rolled to just above the elbow. Still, he looks
better than he feels. Between the files and Milena's wine, he slept
maybe an hour.

On the third floor he waves at the other die−hards.
Wendolyn of course, the head of the LatAm team. She's there
every Saturday, even some Sundays. Julissa, her assistant, nods
from the printer room. Stepan, Group Legal Counsel, lifts a royal
hand from his corner office opposite the hall from Luis's.

"Ciao, bicho."

Luis opens the door wider. "Jesus, Stepan. You
experimenting with cryogenics in here?"

Stepan sits back and his chair creaks. "Blasted heat. Every
morning I consider suicide. Or a transfer to Luxembourg."

Luis sets the binder on Stepan's desk. "I vote Luxembourg. None of this bullshit there."

"Nowadays? Everyone has US investments. No escape from FATCA."

"But in Luxembourg – anywhere, actually, except here – they make their clients provide proof of tax residency." Luis jiggles the binder, a little tap–dance on the desk.

Stepan looks out at the Caribbean morning glittering outside. "When I started here – I'm talking years, not decades – dude could come in off the street with a driver's license and a suitcase of money, and we'd set up an investment structure for him. Any trust company would."

"The good old days. Right." Luis presses his eyeballs until fireworks bloom under his lids. "Stepan, OECD directives started back in the seventies. How did you people slip under the radar?"

"The whole Caribbean did. How?" Stepan snorts. "Isn't it obvious?"

"Offshore means, or meant, unregulated. Not sloppy. This," Luis makes the binder dance again, "is sloppy. Negligent, even."

"Well, then." Stepan peeks over his wire–rimmed glasses at Luis. "Isn't it lucky Ehrlich has you. Tackle one of these a week, I'd say you're fully booked for the next, oh, five years."

"We don't have five years. Ehrlich or me. The FATCA deadline is April."

"Better get to it, then. Find anything?"

"Bunch of trust deeds, not slapdash enough to be sham, but close. And bank accounts. Everywhere. Ehrlich isn't a signatory in any of them, apparently."

"Pity." Stepan sighs. "I left the evaluation of the other files on your desk. Did Milena say how we'll proceed?"

Luis feels his armpits dampen. "We, uh, didn't go into that. But she'll approve."

"Sure?"

"Why wouldn't she? It's win–win. The client, Ehrlich, the –"

"IRS?"

"Not if there's no US persons involved."

Stepan blinks at him.

"Stepan. Fuck. I thought that was policy here. No US persons as clients."

"Without proof of tax residency, how can I – or anyone – assert that?"

"See no evil?" Luis's stomach is on a wild ride.

Stepan chuckles. "Plausible deniability. Let's get to work, bicho. Make the fiduciary world a better place and all."

Luis thought his stints in Hong Kong, Guernsey, Wall Street – Wall *Street* – would've prepared him for anything. Those big financial centers are paradise. Here, in the cradle of the trust industry, it's just a step up from the abacus. From quills and inkwells, a cowled monk recording transactions in spiky longhand. At least there's computers. With Windows; welcome to the future. While his boots up, Luis swigs the last of his cappuccino and starts on Stepan's report.

Source of wealth declaration says inheritance. But where's the backup? No will, a faded death certificate, copy of a copy, and not notarized. A certification stamp on a corner, a scrawl over it. He turns the page to study it. M. Durant. Milena; it figures.

An hour later, when MD herself – how apropos: her initials also stand for Managing Director – pops into his office, he's turned Stepan's three pages into a twelve–page litigation dossier.

"Good morning, Luigi. Again."

He looks up. "Sorry I left so early. I had to –"

"Don't. I hate excuses." She saunters in on six–inch slingbacks, pointy things with red daisies fragile enough to be made of glass, certainly too fragile to carry Milena's curves. She sits a thigh on the corner of his desk, pushes the to–do tray away, leans over the report. It's on purpose, all of it: the skirt riding up, the twist from the waist so her ass looks rounder and her cleavage shows just enough swell. He knows this, and still that non–discriminating entity between his legs twitches in appreciation. He glances across the hall, but Stepan has his back to them.

"This is wrong, Luigi."

"Sloppy, yeah. Negligent too."

But Milena is giggling. "No, honey. This one," she points to a triangle in the structure diagram, "Almeida N.V. That's the only entity domiciled in Curaçao. All the others aren't. The audit doesn't include them."

"They're part of the client's structure. We need to –"

"No. We disclose what we're required to disclose. We do not volunteer information."

"But –"

She grazes his cheek. "You didn't shave?"

"Milena, listen. FATCA isn't a game. Once Curaçao signed that exchange of information agreement, all fiduciaries operating under a Curaçao license are bound, by law, to provide the declarations –"

"And we will. But the request is for entities domiciled in Curaçao. Until the IRS learns to widen the scope of their requests, we provide only the information they ask for. Not a goddamn byte more. Are we clear?"

The upbraiding stings like a bitch slap. "Yes ma'am."

She puts a palm back on his cheek, ignores the bristle this time. "Don't pout. I'm just training my replacement."

He ignores the impulse to recoil. "Is it official?"

"That I'm leaving next year? I already signed the Singapore contract."

"That I'm your replacement."

Milena's red mouth purses. "Potentially. Is that enough?"

Luis trails a finger over the contour of her knee. "For the moment."

"A threat?" But she's laughing. "If you don't get to be MD you'll – what? Leave?"

"There'd be nothing to stay for."

"You could come to Singapore."

He laughs too. These things are best approached disguised in humor. "As your lapdog? Enticing."

She tweaks his ear, a tad too hard. "Speaking of. How's the monster mongrel?"

No trouble smiling for real this time. "Dog food is bankrupting me."

She turns away, fiddles with his computer, clicking through the open programs. "You should take him to the shelter."

The feel−good lasted all of three seconds. Maybe Milena does it on purpose. "Nah. We're good, Al and I."

Her laughter is sharp, the one she uses with novice account managers. "Does he call you Betty?"

The Paul Simon association never occurred to him. Creatively challenged as he is, he'd planned to call the dog Guy. Then, for reasons he doesn't think about much, a fragment of poetry started looping in his head as he drove to the vet that first time. *Let us go then, you and I / When the evening is spread out against the sky.* One more thing Al can be grateful for. He could've spent the rest of his days answering to Pru. "It's for Prufrock. You know. The Love Song of Albert J."

"Whose song?"

He almost says the lines out loud. Suddenly he doesn't want to share it, another piece of his soul for her to play with. "An old poem. Doesn't matter."

"Isn't poetry wasted on a dog? Seems to me your Pure Frock might be better served recited to me. Over Chablis and sushi on the beach? I have a bottle cooling in the car. You get the sushi?"

If he had a tail, it would be expected to wag. "I've got hours to go here."

"But I just cut today's workload by −" She glances at the structure diagram. "By five. Come on, it's too beautiful a day."

"One condition."

She's already at the door. "No Al, Luigi."

He thinks of the dog's forlorn face at the window, the joy when Luis comes home. But this due diligence project is the key to getting out from under Milena — figuratively and otherwise. "No, no Al. But hear me out on the FATCA thing. You're right about the scope of the IRS request. But Ehrlich can't function, not anymore, without tax residency certificates. For every entity."

Her lacquered fingernails tap against the pressed wood. "Fine. This once. Then you promise to never bring it up again."

"Just — hear me out."

A Chablis and sushi miracle. That's what Luis needs.

Sunday, 2nd February 2014

La Ronde / Gina and Joey

by Townsend Walker

Joey, it's Gina.

Gina?

Your sister, you smuck.

I got a sister?

Okay, I get the message. It's been a while. But with things, you know how it is.

No, I don't know.

Look, I'm very sorry I haven't called you. I apologize. I should be nicer to my older brother.

I'm starting to hear you, but lighter on the older bit.

So how are you?

Not bad, moving business is good, the economy, house prices up, lot of people decamping to Florida, permanently now. Last two winters have been a bitch – Hurricane Sandy, then the big power outage. Sonia is keeping busy with Mama and her round of doctors. Kids are finally getting good grades. Put them in a school run by nuns. They know how to crack the whip.

Been there; felt it. Hey did you hear? Punxsutawney Phil didn't see his shadow this morning, short winter we're gonna have.

You called to tell me about a groundhog? I don't think so. What do you want from your big brother that your big rich daddy can't give you?

You remember Madge? You went out with her moons ago. When we were at Barnard I fixed you up. The blonde, big brown eyes, built.

Madge? Oh, yeah. I remember Madge.

There something you're not telling me, Joey?

Sounds like she never did either.

What?

There was more than one date; we went out from Christmas til I graduated and left for San Fran.

But she was stuck on some guy from Rome. They'd go off somewhere every weekend. Never let any of us meet him.

Giancarlo Falcone?

How do you know?

That was me.

You? My brother.

All those stories of Latin romance she carried back to the dorm were made up in a tiny room we had in Little Italy; well, some were made up.

You jerk. You're both jerks – my brother and my best friend. I don't believe it.

So ask her.

Look, I called because she needs help.

What kind?

Her husband runs around and –

So?

beats her, loses the kids, believe that? And there's a pre nup.

Where's this going?

She wants to get rid of him.

So why do the two of you need my help getting her a divorce.

Divorce is not the kind of *rid* she's thinking about. She's thinking of a permanent *rid*.

Why doesn't she buy a gun? Not like they're hard to find. Shoot the bastard the next time he goes after her.

So what if he grabs her and the gun is in the other room, huh? Or, you remember that woman in South Carolina? She shot her husband as he came through the door with a bat. She didn't wait for him to hit her with it before she pulled the trigger. She ended up in prison. Some kind of justice that is.

But you're calling me, because?

You used to hang around with Uncle Tony, who used to hang around with people who know about these things.

Whoa. It's been a long time since I've seen Uncle T. We went sideways on a deal couple of years ago. So no. Can't help you there.

Come on, you gotta know somebody.

Why I gotta know somebody?

Joey, Joey, you always know people. Madge is in a real pickle. I saw her day after she got beat up. Make up couldn't cover it up. She limped out of the bar. It was brutal. I cried and cried. I would of done Frank myself if I knew how. Think about it, please.

Hold on a sec. Got another call coming in. Bidding on a big job. Moving the Pru to a new building near the Newark airport.

I'm back.

How's Mama? She better?

Yeah, she's doing fine.

I hope so. The fall certainly didn't help her any.

How long you gonna go on about that? My wife goes out for an hour and Mama picks that time to try to get out of bed and make coffee, something she's never done in her life. When we're here she won't get out of bed unless someone is there by her side. I might fall. I might this. I might that. It wasn't Sonia's fault.

Sure, it was Mama's.

Look, you're not here with Mama. We are. Sometimes you gotta get out of the house. The constant yammering, bitching. You'd think she was little Red Riding Hood: too hot, too cold, too salty, but never ever right.

You telling me about my mother? My mother? All I hear from your dear Sonia ... do you know I get three e-mails a week from her complaining how I don't do enough for my mother, how I don't see her. And that doesn't count those she sends to our sisters and not me. Christ on the cross!

Gina, let's not get into that, huh? Sonia, well you know how she is. It's just when Mama's going off.

Sonia blabs on to Lucy and Carol about what I don't do and then I hear from them about how I'm mistreating our mother. It's like everyone's happy to take the money, but if I'm not there every day I don't get any points. In fact, it means I hate her. Since we moved up to Greenwich it's at least an hour each way and that's if nobody's on the Cross Bronx. When did that ever happen? I get sick, sick to my stomach and it's because of Sonia.

What do you want me to do about it? Tell my wife that she's upsetting my sister. Somehow that is not going to work. But I swear whenever she goes negative, I stick up for you. And that's not easy sometimes. Just ignore her. Delete the emails.

But it hurts, Joey. She's turning the family against me. Any little spark, she's there with a gas can.

Sec. Hey Soni, can you get the door. I'm on the phone ... with Gina ... yeah, I'll tell her. Sonia says hi.

I'll bet.

So Madge?

Did I mention how much she's willing to pay? Fifty big ones.

For that I think I could do some looking around. Guy I used to know, name of Max.

Max Fiori?

No, another Max. Probably still in the business, or knows who is.

24

So you'll let me know.
Yeah, I'll let you know.
And you'll talk to Sonia?
Yeah, I'll talk to Sonia.
So I'll tell Madge Giancarlo is taking care of it.
Yeah, tell her that.
Bye, lover boy.
That was a long time ago.

Five minutes later.

Yo, Gina, so what's this guy's name and what's he look like? Be kind of useful to know.

Name is Franklin Lancaster Cabot III; goes by Frank. Works at Goldman Sachs on West Street, downtown. Six foot three, 200 pounds, perpetually tanned (some gel he uses), curly black hair going gray, beak for a nose, Brooks Brothers dresser, loafers with tassels. And Hermes ties, you know, the silly patterned ones. Outside, Prada Aviators, high end sunglasses, blue tint, all seasons.

Be back. Love ya.

Monday, 3rd February 2014

A Visitor

by Derek Osborne

"Ahoy the boat!"

They're still in Miami, waiting to leave for a month—long shoot on Nantucket. It won't be a pleasant sail this time of year so Max is fine with hanging out while they wait for the contract. The marina's been footing the bill; the little boutiques near the dock have also chipped in. *Gadabout* makes for a great attraction.

"Ahoy the boat," Max hears again. He's been taking more naps these days. It's always pleasant up on deck after the morning rains and before it gets too hot. The bouts of fatigue are getting more frequent so he's been doing any heavy work first thing and then resting after. The tests up in New York went off as planned. It was good to see his daughters. The youngest, Andi, is going to NYU. His sister was there as well, armed with special diets and brochures from other clinics, recommendations for second and third opinions. "Pam," Max had said, "We haven't even gotten the first." But that was his sister.

"Hell—lo—oh?" he hears the person on the dock say again. The voice sounds familiar. It's probably the woman from the photography studio. Max is lounging in the cockpit. It's upholstered in deep green ultra—suede and quite comfortable, his favorite place to nap, and now she's woken him up.

"Come aboard," he says, not bothering to rise. His body is still feeling sluggish, he needs more sleep. Blame it on a Monday.

They ran a new halyard this morning and Eddie had to go up the mast. Hoisting him took its toll. Max closes his eyes again, what's another minute?

"Aren't we the lazy bones."

It's not the photographer. The voice, up close, is unmistakable, the hint of Chilean accent, the studied enunciation of someone who learned English later in life, all of it wrapped in that sexy confidence, the "it" Katherine Hepburn spoke of, as if every word is newly minted just for him. The sound of her voice is spreading a warm, wonderful calm through every discomfort he's feeling, every cell in his body taking a long, deep breath, letting it out with a sigh. He can't help but smile.

"I'm afraid if I open my eyes you won't be there."

"But I am," Rebecca says, "and it wasn't easy coming here."

Something's wrong. Max opens his eyes. She's wearing soft, loose fitting cotton pants and a pale blue tee that somehow manage every curve of her body, her hair tucked under a Yankees cap, dark glasses screaming – *Leave me alone.*

"You never called," she says, pulling off the glasses.

Max wants to laugh. It's a bad habit, imagining conversations three or four lines ahead, life as if it were all some B–Grade movie – a way to avoid, his wife used to say – he starts to sit up.

"No," she says, "don't."

This is not what Max has imagined. True, he never called after the wrap party last month. He'd started to, several times, but he wanted to wait for the tests.

"Becca."

"I told you to call me Becky."

That night at the party he'd called her Becca, it just seemed to fit, the effect had been startling.

"I don't want to call you Becky."

"I can't stand when you call me that …"

Max can't believe what he's seeing. She's crying. It's so adorable he just wants to hold her and let it come. He starts to get up and she takes a step back.

"I mean it, Max … I mean it. I came here to tell you this isn't going to work. I know, it sounds crazy, we haven't even had the 'It' part of it yet and I'm already playing 'It' out and I know how 'It's' going to end …"

"That's a lot of 'Its'."

"Don't make jokes."

"I'm sorry."

Another bad habit.

"You don't know," she says, "it's this god damn business. You're surrounded by so many people who want something from you and … it's lonely, and then this great guy comes along like some fucking life raft and all you want is to never let go and NO!" she says, backing away as Max tries to get up, "I mean it, don't come near me. It's best just to end things now and I can at least imagine what it might have been like to …"

"To what …"

"Just please don't get up. I have to … I have to go."

And before he can she bolts, leaping over the rail and landing on the dock like a cat, like she does on the show, not even bothering with the boarding block. Max is forgetting she does her own stunts.

"Becca," he says.

But she's already down the dock, walking quickly, her arms out wide and stroking back and forth like people do when they exercise. There are others there on the pier, people on the dock, people on their boats. Maybe that's what she wants them to think. She's put the glasses back on.

"Becky," Max calls. She slows but doesn't stop. A hand comes down, low with the palm facing down, let it be for now, she seems to be saying. She doesn't turn.

"We're not done," Max says, but only the boat can hear.

They're far from done. He's watching her now, waiting to see if she'll turn. She's almost out to the parking lot, walking up the long steel ramp.

"Turn around," he says.

She's reached the top.

"Come on, Becca, turn around."

There's this heavy white gate and a chain link fence. They lock it after sunset. She's pushing the gate open, lingering.

"Take your time."

Just then the SAT phone rings. Most of his friends are sailors and they're scattered all over the globe. He looks at the little screen calling out the ID, the latitude and longitude location of the call. "Of course," he says, pushing the TALK button and bringing it up to his ear, "please hold."

"Max, don't hang up…"

It's Pam, his sister. Rebecca has turned around. She can see him there with the phone, and now he can see her digging into one of her pockets and pulling out her own.

"Shit, she thinks I'm calling her."

"What?" his sister says.

"Pam, hold on."

Max is digging out his own cell. He's had Rebecca on speed dial ever since the night of the party. It's already buzzing.

"Hi," he says to the phone.

"You tried to call?"

"Yes, I tried to call."

Now he's holding a phone in each hand, the big SAT phone and the sexy iPhone. His sister is running on but he can't make it out. Pushing the speaker button on the SAT phone, he lifts the iPhone back to his ear.

"Rebecca, let's slow this down."

"What?" his sister says.

"Yes, Max, I agree."

"What's your schedule like?"

There's a pause.

"I'm home the rest of the day."

"Not you, Pam."

"I have to fly out to LA," Rebecca says, "That's why I came down to see you."

"So how 'bout we talk next week?"

"No, we have to talk now. Are you docking the boat again?"

"Who is that?" Rebecca asks.

"My sister, she's on the other phone."

"Who are you talking to?" Pam says.

"My girlfriend," he says to his sister, "We're having our first quarrel."

"Max, you're dating? Oh, that's great. Who is she?"

"Rebecca Vasquez."

"Yeah right."

"Max?" Rebecca says.

"Yes?"

"That felt nice."

He looks down at the face on his phone. He'd taken the photo the night of the party. It's from the side and she's looking down. The camera flashed and she lifted her eyes. "Gotcha," he'd said that night, "Gotcha Becca." That's when he saw the look on her face.

"So we'll talk next week?" Max says.

"No, we have to talk now!"

"God damn it, Pam, shut up for just one minute."

"There's someone else?" Rebecca says.

"No! I didn't mean you."

"I'm teasing."

"Are you talking to me?" his sister says.

He's holding both instruments out in front of him, arm's length, looking from one to the other.

"Pam, you need to wait just a moment, okay?"

Putting the iPhone back to his ear. He's standing now at the stern of the boat, out on the great, wide deck, looking up at her there by the gate.

"Becca?"

Why not? What if the chance never comes? He knows these things; knows how quickly life can come. "Becca …" he begins.

"Max, don't," she says, cutting him off, hearing it in his voice, "Not over the phone. I want to see your face. I want you to see mine."

He knows she's right. He knows she's going to be right about a lot of things from now on.

"Come back here, now," he says.

"No, there's something I have to do."

"Becca ..."

"Think of me?"

"Are you kidding?"

He watches her put the phone in her pocket. She waves, closing the gate. A red, M650 convertible pulls up. It's Anja, her assistant. Talk about hiding in plain sight. Her car flickers in and out of the masts and the other boats lining the pier, running beside the little white shops. There's traffic out on the boulevard.

"Max," his sister is saying, "Max?"

He picks up the SAT phone.

"Yes, Pam, what is it?"

"I just called to see if you got back the tests."

Tuesday, 4th February 2014

A Precise Science

by Gloria Garfunkel

Bipolar Ralph here. Chloe and I are on the last day of our fabulous ski vacation in Park City Utah. We are both incredibly excited to ski powder instead of the slush and ice they call snow in New England. I spend the nights while she's sleeping perfecting my Quality Assurance Data reports. No room for error there.

"Boy," she says, "I didn't realize Quality Assurance was such a demanding and complicated field. I thought it was just fabricated busywork bullshit full of arbitrary numbers to intimidate employees into thinking they are being watched and empirically measured."

"It's a precise science. You've no idea. It's like being a psych. nurse only for a whole organization." Chloe is a psych. nurse for one unit which I admit is worse.

This morning, Chloe says, "Ralph. I think you're bipolar like my father was. You need to get help before a disaster." Her bipolar father had committed suicide.

"Right," I say. "Me bipolar? I just have energy cycles. Is everyone with energy cycles bipolar?"

"Yes, in fact," she says.

And by the way, I am seeking help and take Lithium and I'm still cycling, though you should have seen me before the Lithium. I just don't want Chloe worrying about me. She's been through enough in her life. She being a psych. nurse, really, we both know I'm not fooling her at all. Besides, I know she's gone through all my pills in the medicine cabinet. Truthfully, I'm on a lot more than just Lithium. That's the big gun, so to speak, the 'Anti–Suicide Pill'.

"I'd really like us to talk about this," she says.

"I'd really like not to," I say. "I'm OK. I'm taking care of myself. Don't worry. I'm not your father. I would never commit suicide. He was much worse. He was Bipolar I and I'm Bipolar II."

She gets very quiet and still. I want to hug her, but I can't. But then I do and we both cry.

"I was twelve when he did it and I just thought if I'd been a better daughter …"

"I know."

Crying is not a good sign. I am headed for a downslide.

Ochre

by John Wentworth Chapin

Esther fidgets. She's used to sitting still in bed; she's been bedridden for two months, her multiply–fractured legs mending from the accident, seven metal pins in both. The sheets aren't as clean as they could be, but at least she is out of the hospital. Sitting still to recover is one thing; sitting for a portrait, however, trying to remain motionless, makes her aware of every square inch of skin, every itch, every regret. The late afternoon light bathes the room in a fickle glow, the color of buttery warmth but cold. Always cold.

"I aim to take a sip of my water, and then I might be ready for a little shut–eye," she says.

He concentrates on the oversized watercolor pad in front of him, daubing greens and mustards, pigments a white boy uses to capture the hues of a light–skinned black woman beset by age and catastrophe. She knows he heard her, because his lips move slightly in response. She takes a sip, tilting the water into her mouth from a tall sports water bottle, resting the bottom against the metal safety bedrail.

"How's the painting coming?" she asks. He still doesn't answer. She wants him to answer, and she considers saying his name to get his attention: *Charles*. That seems too personal, though. He makes a popping sound with his lips which reminds her of her father spitting loose flecks of tobacco from his

34

handrolled cigarettes. The memory firms her resolve. She presses a button on the side of the bed, and with a low hum, the top third of the bed reclines. The late afternoon sun slips from her skin, now illuminating a patch of ochre on a far wall.

"Wait!" he cries.

She's startled by the outburst but keeps her finger on the button. "I need to rest," she says, thinking what a surprising thing the world can be that sitting in bed taxes her to the point of exhaustion.

Charles mutters that he is almost finished, but she is beyond politeness. She agreed to the portrait thinking that the company would be nice. It's worse with him there. The stillness forces her into her own mind, and that's the last place she wants to be. She hasn't been able to listen to music or watch television since the accident, and she's not sure why.

He stares at his painting for a moment, then back at her. He sets down his brush and runs his fingers through his hair, a long, plaintive exhale escaping him. His hair is slightly damp.

The center of each of her fingers is frozen with an implacable chill, and he's sweating.

"It's terrible," he sighs, crossing his arms against his chest.

Ten, twenty, thirty years ago, Esther might have reassured him that it was fine, even without seeing the painting. "Do you want to show it to me?" she asks.

Charles nods. "I do. But my painting teacher said it's not a good idea to show a painting until we're done with it."

"Well, *I'm* done," she says, with finality.

"Do you mind if I use the men's room?" Charles asks.

She's hesitant. *You've become a truly wretched old woman who should up and die when you consider not letting people use your toilet.* She points down the hall and shuts her eyes as he leaves the room.

§

She told at least forty people – police and doctors and lawyers – that she doesn't remember the accident. She told them she was driving down the street and the next thing she knows she's lying in a cold, white room that's so bright it hurts her eyes.

But: she remembers every single moment of driving up onto the sidewalk and plowing down three strangers. Her windshield was sprayed with blood and two bodies, so she couldn't see what she hit when she crashed to a halt, but she remembers the blood spatter and the way a stranger's hand smeared it like a finger painting. She remembers the loud racket of her car's damaged engine clacking and sputtering, then voices screaming and yelling.

It was easier to claim amnesia and blackout. They tested her for brain damage and heart damage. They tested her for drug interactions and drug abuse and alcohol. They did a psychiatric evaluation. They theorized about black ice. They begged her to remember, and she pretended to try.

She couldn't explain what she knew: that she was feeling fine and then suddenly she was doing things she didn't expect to be doing. She didn't want to kill those people, *but she didn't try not to*, either. That's something you don't tell a policeman or a doctor or a lawyer. So she remembers everything, but she doesn't understand any of it. She is beginning to fear that she never will.

Charles holds the unfinished painting out to her, a rough pencil sketch of shapes – bed, head, body – painted in washes of tan and olive. Her vision is not what it used to be, but her first thought is dismay that he swallowed her afternoon yet it looks like he's barely gotten started. Her second thought is that it looks like a seasick gingerbread man.

"What do you think?" he asks.

Esther reaches for her bottle of water and tilts it toward her lips.

"Be honest," he says.

She sips, nodding her head slightly to nudge the liquid through the little nozzle. "How long have you been painting?" she asks.

"You hate it," Charles says.

"I don't like when people put words in my mouth," she snaps.

Charles is chastened. She sees the boy in him, always doing what he's told, and she tucks that away for later.

"This is my first painting," he says. "Outside class, I mean."

He called on her three days earlier, introducing himself as a witness to the accident and explaining that he wanted to paint her because he needed to get over the accident. She didn't understand how a portrait would do that, but in that moment of confusion, she assumed he was a painter. She sees now that his brushes and his little easel are new, and she feels tricked, even though he has done nothing wrong. She imagines more days like today, with the torture that silence and awareness bring.

"I'll be honest with you," she says. "I don't want you to finish it."

After a moment of quiet, Charles says, "I need to do this. I don't know why." When Esther doesn't reply, Charles keeps talking. "I can't get the accident out of my head, so I'm trying new things, like this painting class, and I see your face in the windshield coming at me … I'm so lucky to be alive. You were driving straight at me but …"

This perks Esther up. "You saw me driving? Saw me hit them? What did I look like?"

"It was a quick glimpse. You looked straight at the woman you hit, no reaction on your face. Then she was on the

37

windshield and blocked my view. I thought they'd find you slumped over dead from a heart attack or something."

Esther says, "I didn't see you."

"You looked happy!" he says, remembering this now for the first time, surprising himself.

"I wasn't," she shoots back.

Charles stops himself from answering and takes a sharp breath.

Esther looks at him, carefully, seeing him.

Charles sees her, too.

He says, "Why didn't you swerve? You could have missed her."

"I was not in control of my body," Esther says.

"Then who was?"

"I'm not a religious woman."

"Me neither," he replies.

"This is not a ghost story," she says sharply.

Charles nods vigorously, frowning. "I know, I know. But what happened?"

"The answer is that I don't know." She picks at the thin cotton blanket and looks at the watercolor pad as though she hopes to find an answer there in the swaths of paint. "You come back sometime soon and work on that painting," Esther says, "and we'll talk about it."

"Tomorrow?" Charles asks.

"Not tomorrow," she says. "But soon."

Thursday, 6th February 2014

Avoidance

by Lynn Beighley

I'm in my robe, my feet are up, and I'm watching that new show with the smart, snarky, gorgeous city woman who is trying to survive in the male—dominated world of bull riding.

In each episode this happens:

Kristen, our heroine, encounters anger and prejudice because she, a woman, chooses to intrude on man's world.

Jed, the enlightened but sexy cowboy who was brought up by his strong, lesbian grandmother, played by Betty White, argues with her about her actions, but with an intense, obvious sexual tension beneath the encounter.

Her supportive gay rodeo clown friend, Zeke, provides comic relief and emotional support, while also expressing how hunky he finds Jed.

In tonight's awful episode, she jumps into the ring to distract a bull before he can maul Zeke. And now Jed is yelling at her, and she's yelling back at him. And suddenly they're kissing. This is the first time they've kissed, and I know it's predictable, but as corny as it is, it gets to me. I'm a sucker for romance, even predictable romance.

And then, of course, there's a commercial. I look down at the notebook on my lap. I open Facebook and get a shock. Sitting on my lap is a picture of my dad in a cherry red Speedo. Dad. Speedo. I close my eyes. My stomach is roiling. My old cat,

Pollock, chooses this moment to leap on the couch and does his best to shove my notebook aside to occupy my lap. Normally I'd shoo him off because he drools and is often gassy, but right now I need a moment to consider what I just saw. I close the machine and put it on the coffee table.

Pollock purrs on my lap while I ponder. There's a picture of my dad in a Speedo on Facebook. Is this that big a deal? Yes, yes it is, I tell myself. But okay, it really isn't.

I reach forward and open the notebook again. He's still there, almost all of him. I cringe. It's not that my dad looks terrible, I guess. But it's far more of his skin than I ever want to see. I want to be the kind of person who is open–minded enough not to care that her dad is nearly naked online. No, I'm lying. What kind of person is that? Not me. Okay.

The last time I saw my dad in a Speedo I was 13 and my friends and I had just finished swimming in our pool in the backyard. He came out wearing a baby–blue Speedo and my friends started giggling and my face felt like it was on fire and I ran inside to complain to my mother. That evening after yet another huge fight, my mother made him agree to never wear a Speedo again.

This sounds bad. My dad's not like that. I mean, he didn't have any skeevy motive in wearing a Speedo around a bunch of little girls. No, he didn't. He just liked Speedos. Likes Speedos, apparently.

It has 23 likes, his photo. And 13 comments. Above it, he's written, "What do U think of this as my profile picture for online dating sites?" He's using online dating sites now? He types "U" instead of "you"?

I open the comments to see what the consensus is. Several older women I don't recognize have posted things like "ooh baby! I wish Henry looked like you" and "sexxaay <3 <3 <3".

I look away, that's all I can take. Now I'm wondering how I can get him to take this picture down without ever having to actually discuss it with him. I can't even imagine bringing it up.

Until they divorced, I was always able to get my mother to get him to not be so ... out there.

Then I think that maybe it's not a big deal. He's lonely, right? I wonder what sort of mature woman will respond to this picture.

I hear a voice I recognize. I look up and there's Bill Plover, my coworker, on my TV in all his Ploverness. It's a commercial for *You Tell Me*, the reality show he's going to be on that begins next month. I'd like to forget about his show, but nearly every day at work someone brings it up because a big component of this show is romance, and the office thinks that awkward Bill loves me.

"It's up to you what happens. Everything from what to wear to who to date. Everything," the voice says, "and they'll have to do it."

My phone rings, and Pollock farts.

Friday, 7th February 2014

Freak's Father

by Andrew Stancek

Yeah, I'm the freak's father. That's what the tabloids call me.

Wingy. That's what they call him. They covered his story from every angle, making him into a monster, a fraud, a savior, and everything in between, and then they move their scavenging tentacles on those around him, so they can sell more papers. I'm not all that interesting, I don't think, but then again I never thought he was all that interesting either.

You know I never saw the least sign of battiness in him when I still lived with him and his mother. He was a kid like any other, not particularly athletic, kind of nerdy, enjoyed chess and stamp collecting more than baseball. Soccer is my game, understandable for someone who spent most of his life in Europe, and I kicked a ball around with him sometimes. He wasn't disgraceful but he tripped over his feet trying to dribble and didn't throw himself on the ground to catch a ball when he was goalie. I always thought he only came out to please me and would have preferred to be inside reading, or whatever. He was relieved when I said we'd go in for a beer and a lemonade. We weren't terribly close, ever. No, it's not tabloid material. I didn't abuse him and he didn't shoot me with an improperly stored weapon. That's what *The National Conspirer* and *Full Moon* would like. But our past holds no smoking gun.

I moved out when he was bed—ridden with Perthes disease. Does that make me a terrible creep? Maybe. He was in traction for almost two years, then the surgery and his life—changing breakthrough, his flying, merging, modern day Icarus, all that. But you know his story, you don't need me to tell you his. I'm talking about myself here. The timing of my leaving home could have been better, sure. Yveta and I hadn't been getting along for years, not fighting much but not having much use for each other either. It was most likely going to end in divorce no matter what. And then he got sick, really sick, our Adam. Maybe in some families that leads to bonding, and patched up conflicts, and the couple lives happily ever after. All I can say is that didn't happen to us. Yveta was more tense, more tired, more preoccupied with him, Adam. I was suddenly walking the dog three times a day and Scruffy was the only one whose tail wagged when he saw me. Then the dog died, ran into traffic, and whether I was there or not made no difference to anybody. I wasn't looking for trouble, looking to leave, but trouble has a way of finding you, even if you're not looking. The dullest, commonest story: my new secretary broke up with her live—in, at a bar after work she listened to my whining and I listened to hers and it seemed life with her would be better than what I had at home. She wasn't even pretty, kinda mousy really, but she was there and for a while she listened. I moved out, shacked up with her, and less than a year later that was over, too. The charm was pretty thin. But I didn't go back to Yveta and Adam, either, saw no point in that. I wasn't going to eat crow for leaving.

You could say this is the first time I ever really apologized. I've cried into my beer and had a pity party lots of times, of course. But apologized to Adam, no, I've never done that. He's famous now, some would say notorious, but that's not the reason for my apology. I don't want anything from him, no money, not even reflected glory.

I'm looking at my life, reconsidering. I was in a car accident, fractured a fibula, a concussion shook me up, maybe knocked some sense into me. Two of my friends died in the last year. It's Friday today and I'd like to go and knock back a few but there's no one whose jokes I haven't heard a hundred times. What do you really have in life? What is it all about? I'd like to have a better relationship with Adam. Maybe I can still share something with him, maybe he wants to know, maybe he cares.

Everybody wants to learn how to fly like he does. I'm glad he stepped back from all the glory a bit, that he's not on the front covers of every magazine any more, on every TV show. He needs to take stock, too, decide what is right, right for humanity but also right for him. This isn't a patent we're talking about, but a human being. All the yelling and screaming, the controversies, the certainties about what he has to do and how. Well, he's the only one who can decide. He doesn't belong to the world or to a government. He is only himself.

Maybe he wants a father back. Maybe we can do things together. Some fathers fly a kite with their sons. We never did that. Maybe we can fly together, spread our wings, father and son.

Talk to me, Adam. Talk to me, son.

I am sorry.

Saturday, 8th February 2014

Consequences Need Action

by Rachel Ambrose

"I don't know, Isa," I say into the phone. It's cradled between my neck and shoulder as I'm washing dishes in the sink, and I've been talking long enough that my shoulder is starting to ache. "I like Charlotte, but she comes in late and she leaves her stuff everywhere and her cat likes to knead his claws on my comforter."

"I told her to get rid of that damn cat," Isa replies, and I can hear the sigh in her voice. "Look, Claire, it's just a few more months. I'll be back after that, and you won't have to pick up her dirty panties anymore." She pauses as I chuckle into the phone. "College roommates don't change, you know."

I quickly hang up after Charlotte walks in the kitchen. She's taller than me, with bright eyes and brown hair that she dyes varying shades of green and blue. She works in a restaurant as a sous chef, so she's gone a lot, which is a great perk as far as I'm concerned. Mondays and Tuesdays are her days off, and sometimes she cooks for us. She doesn't go to the grocery store much, but she brings home food from her restaurant and that's good enough. Tonight she's humming and shimmying around in a slinky black dress. "Where are you off to?" I venture. Sometimes my voice seems like a squeak in my throat.

"Oh, this birthday party for one of my friends at Bubble, I got the night off work specially," she replies. I've heard of

Bubble; it's a champagne bar in the artsy downtown district. "You're welcome to come if you want, the more the merrier." She shoots me a smile that almost cracks on the edges it's so sweet. I consider it for about half a second, and then it occurs to me that I'd have to get out of my sweatpants if I did go.

"I don't like champagne," I say. There's a moment of disappointment in her face, but she hides it quickly. "And I don't know any of your friends, I'd feel awkward."

"They're awesome!" she says. "You should come, even if you don't like champagne. Come on, I bet you have something cute in your closet." She bounces on her heels to my room and I follow her reluctantly. "You won't even have to stay long if you drive yourself!" she says. "We haven't been out on the town as roomies since I moved in." She's wheedling me, and I know I might mess up the subtle and delicate harmony of our roommate–ship if I refuse. I roll my eyes at her black–sequined back, but say, "Yes, okay, I'll come. You can't leave me in the corner with a whiskey and soda, though."

She makes a noise that conveys far more excitement than I think the situation merits. "This'll be so much fun!" She starts going through my closet, but stops abruptly after I clear my throat. "I'll, uh, let you get ready then. Take your time!"

"Sorry," I say. "I just don't like people going through my stuff except for me."

"No, no!" she says, beating a hasty retreat out of my room. "It's cool! Come out when you're ready to go."

I emerge, finally, a torturous twenty minutes later after wrestling myself into a bright blue sheath dress that I'd forgotten I borrowed from a cousin. I run a wet brush through my hair. Makeup's for people who actually give a shit, I decide, as I shuffle through my shoes and remind myself that bunny slippers aren't an acceptable public footwear choice. I settle on some white flats, grab my wallet, and decide that I'm just going to have to suck it up and have a good time. The horror.

We slip into Charlotte's car and head off downtown. The trees are festooned with little yellow lights like the kinds you see at old carnivals and fairs, and the sky is blue like my dress. I tug at it as she puts the radio on scan. "You'll like Blake," she says as we pull up to the parking lot. "He's really sweet, he's a painter and we go back since before college." I just hope that the drinks aren't too expensive.

As we walk in, the dark heat of the bar envelops me and reminds me of being wrapped in a comforter. I can deal with this, I think, as I wave a little to Charlotte's friends as she introduces me. There's Katie and Kevin, a real estate agent couple, and Ralph, a food truck owner, and Jason, a couples therapist. My lowly "administrative assistant" job title seems so sophomoric compared to their polished careers. And finally there's Blake himself, a short dark–haired guy with a smudge of green paint on his nose and hazel eyes. I know I don't get out a lot, but I can't stop staring at him in his black button–up shirt with the sleeves rolled up to the elbows, exposing lightly muscled forearms. He smiles at me and I see his teeth have a gap in front, and I have to swallow down my hard–beating heart. I take a champagne glass from Charlotte and we stand and toast Blake's birthday, and I gulp down the drink and nearly choke on the hidden cherry at the bottom. I try not to make a face at how sweet it is.

"I haven't been out in a while," I find myself joking to Blake. "Even drinks keep trying to kill me." What is this? I don't quip. You can't call me witty. Instant Human: Just Add Champagne? Good to know. I immediately order another, taking care this time to remember about the stealthy fruit.

"I know what you mean," Blake says, nodding and sipping from his glass. "Some days it doesn't seem like I can physically leave the house." Are we secretly the same person? I wonder. We talk about his paintings and how landscapes can capture emotion, and his eyes seem to glow as I drink more (did I mention I haven't had more than a glass of wine in one go in over a year?). I'm on my third glass when Charlotte taps me on the shoulder. "Don't monopolize the birthday boy, honey," she says, grinning, but there's ice behind that warmth. Does she have a thing for Blake? I can't tell. Does Blake have a thing for her? I suddenly feel the need to sit down. Being social is hard work.

We eventually leave and head to a pancake restaurant, where Blake and I manage to make everyone else feel like third, fourth, fifth and sixth wheels, which may set a new world record. Kevin and Katie head out before the food hits the table, and the others sit there poking at their waffles and coffee, reminding me of petulant children. Blake tries to draw the others into our conversation, but no one else quite seems to grasp what we're talking about (what are we talking about?) and I'm having too much fun to care about stepping on toes. We exchange numbers as we're leaving and he makes my insides do a cartwheel when he leans in close and brushes a rough kiss against my cheek. "It was a great birthday, thanks to you," he says, and he smells like woodsmoke and citrus and male and oh boy. I sweep into the car with Charlotte sitting silently beside me and burble, "Man, I am *gone*," and I don't think to explain which definition of "gone" I mean, because I kind of mean all of them at once.

Sunday, 9th February 2014

Valentine's Lay

by Gill Hoffs

If I don't stick it in, I might leak. He said 'smart casual', so black trousers are fine, but I know from the preference form he left with the agency that tight tops and bared midriffs are what he's hoping for from our girls, so something long and drapey from the 'camel toe coverups' section in my wardrobe is out. I could stick it in my bag beside the candle and matches and hope for the best, trim the string like when I was a stripper and hope a handjob will hold him off, maybe offer my arse, or even call in sick and let Pamela take my role.

But I like my job, I like him. Never mind the loafers and too short trousers; I want to go on this date.

I stick the paper bullet in my bag, down a half–pint of orange juice, and go for a shower then take my tweezers to the topiary heart between my legs, and make sure the edges are tidy. I can feel the orange juice working its magic in my intestines and do some sit–ups to help it along.

Ten minutes later and I'm reading up on Mozart as I shit. Arse it is, then.

I've an hour before my taxi arrives in which to choose a final outfit, do my hair and makeup, and floss my teeth. He likes to lick the ones at the front, so I give them an extra scrub before applying scarlet lipstick then get on with the usual faff of mascara (chocolate), eyeliner (black), eye shadow (bronze), concealer (ivory) and blusher (pink). Hair in plaits, one draping each breast with a long thin black ribbon tied round the end. He likes to watch them tickle my nipples when I go on top, then pull the ribbons free and watch my hair loosen as we fuck. I bet he uses my plaits like reins when he takes me from behind.

I pull on a black satin thong, a present from a grateful client last Valentine's Day, then fiddle with its matching shelf bra, my boobs jiggling as I hook the clasp in place. As with Christmastime, Valentine's Day leaves me with too much red–and–black themed nonsense to sensibly handle at home. So unless the underwear, buttplugs, whips and fine chains are something I can use with a client or for my own entertainment, onto eBay they go. I much prefer whipped cream to whips and chain–stores to chains, but if a client is willing to pay for my exceptional services, so be it. Sean just likes a bit of kinky candle play and for me to show up in exotic underwear, though he fancies himself as the new Marquis de Sade. I reckon Sade is more up his street, though a 'smooth operator' he is *not*.

Stockings, suspenders, trousers, heels, stop for a minute and pet the cat. I miss her when I'm working, though I doubt very much that she gives a shit so long as her auto–feeder works. Now for a top. Something that clings and shows the world if I'm cold or not, something that shows my client there are no cups on a shelf bra, just uplift and easy access for fun.

I decide on a clingy red number and pull it on, the deep V neck allowing me to dress without smudging my makeup, the soft fabric showing off my nipples and plaits and leaving a broad band of skin showing around my waist. Then I sit and read a little more about Mozart until the taxi beeps and I grab my bag and umbrella and head out for my 'date'.

§

We're feeding each other sushi and acting like we're in love when his boss walks past our table and halts in a double-take.

"Sean? Hallo! And this must be …?"

I smile angelically at the face above the belly hovering so close to my cheek.

"Donald, hi. Good to see you mate. This is Jennifer. Jennifer, Donald, Donald, Jennifer."

I offer my hand but he leans down for a kiss and a look down my top. We mutter about delight and pleasure and I make like I'm shy but push my elbows into my lower ribs, and Sean's boss stares at my cleavage as his crotch alters and his cock pushes against the fly of his jeans.

"Donald, Jennifer's studying the history of classical music. Jen, Donald's team manager at my work."

"Sean's told me so much about you, I'm so glad to finally put a face to the name."

While I feign enthusiasm, Sean fiddles one-handed with the phone hidden under his napkin. It rings out, and he checks the screen, easing his bulk from the booth while saying, "Sorry, it's important I take this, it's the Wiederman account. Donald, would you …?" and pointing at me.

Donald inclines his head slightly and gestures to Sean to go, then eases himself into the vacant seat. It's a small booth, adequate for two or cosy for three, and he scoots along until his thigh brushes mine under the table.

"I hate to keep you from your wife …" I murmur, and he holds up a hand to stop me.

"Nonsense. It's a pleasure to take care of you, my dear, a pleasure. I'm here with some golfing buddies, anyway, not my wife."

"Sean told me just the other night what a great boss you are. I'm so pleased to meet you and tell you how grateful I am for taking such an interest in his career."

His eyebrows raise a little at this, and I know it's because he does nothing of the sort.

"Well ... he's a good worker. He deserves it."

I lay a hand on his thigh, not so high up or so far in as to be indecent, lean closer, and say, "Still, I appreciate it." I pull in my lower lip with my teeth and murmur, "Really appreciate it."

The next move has to be his. His eyes flick to the side, checking for Sean who said I'd have five minutes tops before his return. I can smell whisky on his breath and perhaps this skews his judgment, I don't know, but one of his hands moves mine up his thigh to his crotch and the other slips up the side of my top closest to him, invisible to anyone who might be watching in the restaurant. I groan quietly and let my eyelids droop a little, still holding his gaze, while he fingers my nipple and damn near drools.

"Jesus ..." he whispers, and I rub his cock through the over-washed denim. It's small enough to be a hardened bollock.

"I'd like to say ... thank you ... properly ... some time ..."

"What for?"

His nostrils are flaring with each inhalation of breath, and I know I have him.

"For Sean's ... promotion."

"But he ... yes. Sometime soon?"

I nod and lick my lips, grateful to the cosmetics industry for long-lasting lip stains. One last rub and I sit back as if I hear someone approaching, Donald's hand slithering down my side and back to normality, away from my tit. Sean takes his cue and returns from round the corner, where he's been monitoring the situation using the mirror behind the bar.

"Sorry about that, Jen. Thanks for looking after my girl, Donald. You know how it is, I just can't seem to leave my work in the office."

Donald scooches over, stands up to let Sean regain his seat, and claps him on the shoulder with an open hand as he does so.

"Sure, no problem. That's some woman you've got yourself there."

Sean winks at me openly.

"Oh, I know. Enjoy the rest of your night."

"Shall do."

Donald catches my eye as he moves away and I smile at him. He hesitates, turns back, and says, "Oh, and Sean? Come see me in the morning. Pleasure to meet you, Jennifer. Hope I see you again soon."

I nod, saying, "I'm sure you will."

Once Donald is away, Sean raises an eyebrow at me. I nod. We finish our drinks and leave.

I drip candlewax in a heart on his chest, my version of romantic, and let Sean spank me with the single red rose (no thorns, thank goodness) he got me for Valentine's Day before I turn around and lower myself onto his cock. No cramps, no warning signs, so fingers crossed I'll make it home before I end up riding the red wave. Up go his hands to the ribbons, and I rock my hips back and forth for a bit before reaching behind me to tickle his balls.

He grabs my arse to rock me harder, and I use my other hand to play with the candle some more.

"Thanks ... for ... the ... promotion."

I wink at him.

"No problem. Happy Valentine's Lay."

Mister Weatherbee

by Susan Tepper

"God is good, God is great, and we thank him for this food. Amen." I make the sign of the cross.

Because somebody, a gift from God, God the father almighty, has cut a hole in the chain link fence surrounding the school yard. And the hole is in a very good place, a God–like place, behind a clump of thick juniper bushes that stay bushy all the year 'round. "Glory be to God in the highest."

Over the weekend I traded in the Dodge for a Buick LeSabre. Or should I say the Dodge went on the scrap metal heap. This Buick is toast–colored. A bit more roomy than the Dart, which makes for more comfort. It has a good back seat. I've lain there, alone, holding my little darling, this one a small black boy with the most exquisite head of curls. I have held him and held him until we both nearly died from the rapture. I cross myself again. "Jesus, our savior and our light, protect us."

Some druggie cut a hole in the fence to find God, too. God has his ways of coming to us all. He comes to me in the form of so many beautiful boys. God led me to this school yard. I could have taken the main highway to get on the parkway, but that day it was detoured on account of road work. It detoured past the school yard. God knows and protects us all if we follow his path.

Yesterday I practiced going through the hole. Tight but doable. I felt like Alice down the rabbit hole. "Frankly, Alice, women don't do it for me." Girls, either. I don't like their stuff it scares me shitless.

I get out of the Buick, lock the door, and crouch down squeezing through the fence hole. It's a cold, damp day. The ground smells like a fresh dug grave. I think about my mother. *So much blood from you we had to throw away the mattress*, she'd say. Smacking my cheek hard. *Cloudy with no chance of sun*. That's what Mister Weatherbee said on the telly this morning. I gauge my days by Mister Weatherbee.

Wedged in the junipers I can see the boys and not be seen. This is much better than being in the car. I can see my little darlings, yet also hear their sweet chirping voices. I love when they make their little bird sounds and squeals. Once their voices change they are of no interest. I want the smooth cheek like the hand of God. The face with its dark down that will turn to a stiff growth – no thanks. I want my baby chicks cuddly smooth and hairless.

My little darling has a name! A real name, not a made–up one by me. I get the goose bumps! Masia some of the others call him. Masia. Could be Egyptian. Or Ethiopian. He's very dark and beautiful, my Masia. Jesus was a black man, too, despite that the Catholics made him into a blue–eyed blond. I have done my research on Jesus. So fuck the pope and the rest of those Catholic dickhead priests. God exists outside of the church. I am God and one with God.

Masia is a panther boy, the way he moves he needs to be in a warm place where the grass is tall enough to cover his movements, where he can slink and slither and no one will ever find him.

A little girl is smiling at him, handing him something. Candy? Masia puts it in his mouth and smiles back. Can he be so easily bought by a girl?

I shift my position in the junipers noticing the blue–gray berries; debating whether they are edible. None of the other little darlings capture my attention the way Masia has. There is all the time in the world. It's been constructed this way. "At the right hand of God the father almighty."

The teachers are scarce today, and only one teacher aide. Is there a strike and these are the scabs? Scabs, because instead of the usual hovering, watching, this group is yapping among themselves, ignoring the kids, talking on their phones, texting. The kids are not being properly watched or handled. It should be reported. If these are scabs they need to find more responsible scabs. It's a travesty what goes on in this world.

When these filthy scabs finally hustle the little darlings back inside, I slip out through the hole. I think about covering it up. Protection is first in line. I will get a slab of wood and cover up the hole. This way only I can gain entrance and exit. I'll figure out a way to latch it to the chain link fence.

At Home Depot I walk the aisles. It's a miserable place. Reminds me of Desert Storm, those Quonset huts the military constructed. What a freaking fuck up. Some of the nurses tried making me there but I put a fast stop to that. One got pissed and called me Candy. Made no bones about the fact that her nose was out of joint.

In the plywood section, I examine several thicknesses. None of the employees wearing the orange aprons show any interest in helping me. "Hey! Some help here!"

An old guy bordering on seventy comes over finally. "Yeah?"

"I need to board up a hole in a chain link fence."

"Wood isn't your answer," he says. "You trying to keep a dog from running away?"

"Yeah, Grandpa, that's the ticket. My bulldog Hairy Pits keeps escaping the yard."

The guy stares at me under long, bushy gray eyebrows trying to figure out if I'm dicking him.

"So what do you think?"

"You need a fence fixer." He walks off.

I push my tongue around inside my jaw. He could be right. It may not be a plywood operation. I decide to leave things go for the time being. *Chance of rain*, Mister Weatherbee said.

Let God do his work and I'll do mine.

Lost and Found

by Jessica McHugh

"Through him, with him, in him, in the unity of the Holy Spirit, all glory and honor is yours, almighty Father, forever and ever."

There was a time when Edward McKenzie's thoughts couldn't stray during the Liturgy of the Eucharist, especially during an event as sacred as a wedding. For years, speaking the ritual's sacred words and hearing his parishioners' passionate replies quickened his heart with joy. Now, he runs on autopilot. It still inspires joy, but he can't deny that it would be tenfold if he could prepare the sacrament with feminine, manicured fingers. He uses the oddity of a Tuesday wedding to justify his distraction, but looking to the young bride and groom, their affection aglow, he can blame no one but himself.

After nearly thirty years of service, Father McKenzie's love in God is not lessened, only his faith in his *right* to serve God. What kind of man can stand in the house of the Lord, the consecrated host at his fingers, and wish, beyond Heaven and Earth, that he were a woman?

A selfish man. A frightened man.

A sinner.

As the bride and groom look up at him in adoration, Edward tries to focus on the task at hand. He lifts the communion paten to his people. Beneath the host, it is freshly polished, shining like the jewelry he's too afraid to wear outside his apartment. The candles are reminders, too. Lit by the altar boys, their scent is similar to his grandmother's perfume, the kind he dabs behind his ears and knees, hoping someone might lean in for a closer sniff. He pours the wine and no longer sees blessed blood. He sees a night of desire, even debauchery, in the chalice, and he aches to scream his truth from the pulpit.

Calm yourself, child. Take a breath and tell Grandma Eleanor what's troubling you.

"No, not here," Edward says, shaking. The chalice tilts in his hand, spilling a drop of wine.

An altar boy sidles up, whispering, "You all right, Father?"

Most of the boys let their hair grow shaggy this time of year, but not Nelson Wade. As usual he's clean—cut, his vestments appropriately pressed for the occasion, and he wears a room—brightening smile that puts most Edward sees to shame.

"Father Edward?"

"Everything's fine, Nelson. Thank you."

More lies in God's house. What has he become? And worse, what will become of him when his wicked life is through? Other people live as they wish without fear of damnation, so part of him believes he could too, but too many evil interpretations from the old days linger in his heart. He wants God to love him no matter his manner of dress or sexual preference, but he grew up believing those desires would earn him a one—way ticket to Hell.

To his parishioners, Edward McKenzie is the mild—mannered minister who lives alone for better religious reflection. He supports the community through charity work, helping to clean up the parks, volunteering at the local soup kitchen, even reading to children at the library, but it isn't a social situation for him.

The reasons are rarely questioned. He thanks God daily for that – and apologizes. God knows his mind and the sinful thoughts filling it. He fears damnation, but fears losing his flock more. He can't imagine remaining their shepherd after revealing he's a wolf in chiffon clothing.

"The Body of Christ," he says to Charlie Kitner, a strapping man who runs the local hardware store.

Charlie whispers, "Amen." When his tongue slides over his bottom lip to catch Christ's love, Edward shivers.

No, he hasn't acted on *every* desire.

The man's lips bend upward. It's as if he knows the glory of the Lord, riveting his soul as the wafer dissolves on his tongue. His pleasure makes Edward's lips do a similar dance – until Sarah Kitner takes her husband's place, her tongue a protruding plank.

Sarah doesn't make Edward's mind wander. The revelation is a knife, especially when he sees how happy communion makes her. Both Kitners. They repeat "Amen" together and clasp hands for their stroll down the aisle. The only time Edward feels that happy is when he's hidden away, his face soft and ivory from his grandmother's makeup, pretending – no, *becoming* – Eleanor. For the Kitners, for the newlywed Barrons and so many of his parishioners, happiness comes easy.

After the service, he cries in the sacristy. Hunched over the desk, his hands clasped in prayer, Edward's tears fall upon the marriage certificate still needing his signature. He dabs it dry with a tissue and signs the paper before setting it aside. They come again, harder.

He's felt post–service sorrow before, but he used to be better at disguising it.

Because you want to tell them the truth. Eleanor crouches beside him and kisses his hand. *Dear child. Would it be so hard?*

He buries his face in his hands, and nods.

Nelson Wade opens the door. Seeing the priest hunched over, his body quaking, he says, "Father, what's wrong? Please don't tell me everything's fine."

Edward wipes away the tears before he turns to him.

"I promise it's nothing you need to worry about," he says. "Is there something I can do for you?"

Nelson holds up a purple tube of lipstick. "Someone left this on one of the pews. I figured I'd drop it in the Lost and Found."

He hands it to Father Edward, who removes the top and spins the lipstick out. It glints under the sacristy fluorescents, too deliciously. He doesn't see Nelson's stare until he rolls down the lipstick. Clearing his throat, Edward slides past Nelson to the jar by the sacristy door. He lifts the lid and drops the lipstick inside. It looks regal atop hair elastics, earrings, and action figures.

"I might know who it belongs to. I can let her know at the next service," Nelson says. "Unless you don't want me to …"

Edward clamps the jar closed, but his eyes don't leave it. "Is there anything else, Nelson?"

The boy shakes his head and closes the door behind him, but his "unless" stays in the sacristy, hanging over Edward like a sweltering, strangling fog. Certain he's alone, he opens the jar again. With the lipstick's pastoral purple winking at him from the Lost and Found, Edward's happiness comes easy.

Wednesday, 12th February 2014

Supermarket Sweep

by Shane Simmons

"Ihaveanewboyfriend!"

I'm pinned against the shelves where the dusty tinned vegetables and soups sit, and despite the fact that we haven't talked to nor seen each other since last month's heated exchange, Sandra wastes no time getting onto bragging about her new bloke.

"Oh, he's gorgeous! I can't believe how perfect he is for me!"

My attention trails off as I pay more mind to the woman with greasy, tied back hair, bent over at the other end of the aisle, concealed from full view by a circle of screeching blonde girls and a pram. I'm certain she's shoving things in amongst the blankets covering a poor kid in the pram.

"Oh you won't believe this!" Sandra reaches over and takes a bottle of vegetable oil down from the shelf behind me. "My sister called. Can you believe she actually called *me*! And, she was hysterically crying!" she cackles. "She's preggers and he's left her! She doesn't even know where he is!" Sandra bursts into a full on belly laugh and startles a nearby pensioner who wobbles dangerously on her sticks.

She skims over the jars of ready–made pasta sauce and says, "I just told her to fuck off and die," before picking one up and dropping it in her basket. The pensioner sneers before she shuffles away, muttering under her breath.

"He must've realised I was a better fuck than that whore. See, things always turn out for the better!" Sandra states. "Karma will always fuck you up."

She bares me the widest grin before walking ahead but I wonder just whether she should be smiling so soon. I'm certain there's a bit of bad karma coming to bite each one of our sorry arses.

"You'll need to meet my new man and give him your seal of approval! We should all go out for dinner sometime!"

I can't think of a better way to spend a night.

"I would invite you around just now but I'm making a romantic dinner for him coming over!"

I examine the contents of her basket. "Spag bol?" It's all she can really cook.

"What else? So, any signs of *lurve* on your horizon?"

My silence and blank stare give Sandra all the answer she needs.

"*Anyway*, I was thinking, with your love life, or rather lack of, you need to get a job in the hospital with me!"

In the short time I've known Sandra she's met every one of her male interests through that place. It's more a free−for−all dating agency than a job. Maybe it's the horrible, baby−poo green uniforms.

"There are *so* many gays! Nurses, porters! You just tell me your type and I'll keep a look−out!" She leans in and whispers, "There are rumours about a few of the surgeons and specialists too! Just imagine, you could bag yourself a well−paid doctor! I've been trying to get one since I started there!" She winks, but I'm certain nothing she's said is in jest.

I open the fridge and take a pint and pop it in my basket, it's all I really came in for. Sandra's basket is overflowing with tasty goodies, garlic bread, pancakes, a tub of Häagen−Dazs for her and her new bloke. There's the milk and a microwave macaroni

63

cheese in mine. I wonder if she's right. Maybe I need someone to cook for. Or even better still, cook for me.

"Spag bol, white, red or rosé?" she asks, scanning over the bottles on the shelves.

"Oh come on, that's easy. Red with red meat."

"I'm sure there'll be plenty of red meat tonight! Oh, that reminds me, johnnies!" She marches away as I'm left rolling my eyes and shuddering.

When we arrive at the tills there's a crowd of people waiting to be served and a few of them are shouting, "Just give them the stuff so we can go!" The greasy woman is stood with her arms folded shouting, "I dun 'ave nahthin'!" at the man blocking her path. The kids around her are deadly silent and I find myself feeling a little embarrassed for them. Just then the door opens and two uniformed police officers walk in.

"Ooh, look at the policeman! God, he's so tall!" Sandra stretches her neck out for a better view.

"You've got a man to make dinner for tonight, you're not meant to look. And I thought I'd seen that woman nabbing stuff earlier, bet you it's all in the pram."

"I was only pointing him out for your benefit!"

"And I know you can't resist a man in a uniform, Sandra."

The officers take the woman's arm and lead her, the pram and her troupe to the back of the store. The policeman is about 6'6" with striking hazel-coloured eyes, a dimpled chin, and tightly cropped dirty blonde hair underneath his hat. Not that I'm checking him out.

"Shouldn't you go tug him and give him a statement?" Sandra winks away as if she has a twitch.

"I'm not tugging any policemen, besides, they have cameras so just be quiet!" I lightly punch her on the arm.

§

We exit the store to find darkness has fallen.

"Oh for fuck sake, where did the time go? I need to get on with this dinner!"

Sandra strides into the road only a few steps down from the zebra crossing and I find myself following her to the blare of a car horn that just misses me as she reaches the other side.

"So, the three of us, we'll sort out something soon, okay?" she puffs. She doesn't wait for the answer and turning on her heel, heads off down the pavement.

"I can't wait Sandra," I mutter to myself, "I can't bloody wait."

Thursday, 13th February 2014

Kia

by Michelle Elvy

Stevie stands just inside the arched doorway, watching Ellie, sitting in her mother's Kia with her head bowed. It's an impossibly yellow car. No one should have a car that color, thinks Stevie. He watches Ellie as people come up the steps past him, each one saying some small nice thing. He nods silently, keeps his eyes on Ellie. The wind is fierce and her window is shut. She's closed off the world and he's not seen her in a month. He does not like recalling the last time he saw her, yet that's all he thinks about when he thinks of her. He sees her now through the fogged–up window as she wipes the end of her nose and blows hard. He sees her pull the tissue away, look at it, put it back in her lap. He wonders if she'll just sit there all day, blowing her nose on that same small scrap of tissue. He wants to go talk to Ellie. He could at least give her the handkerchief in his pocket that his mother gave him. He has a million things he thinks he might say. He has nothing to say.

He thinks maybe he could go stand next to the car and just being there would be enough to help her open the door and step out. He will give her a new tissue for her runny nose and they will walk up the steps together. He knows how she can't get out of the car and get on with the day. He feels the same way, but his parents helped him through the small moments of the morning – his mom laying out a pressed shirt on the foot of his bed and squeezing his hand as he sat up, feeling small and terrible; his dad glancing at him in the rear—view mirror – *You okay?* – as they parked along one of the neat rows allotted for this occasion. His parents had been there all along, through this whole wretched month. He knew Ellie only had her mom, and her mom was a drunk. Still, she'd driven her daughter here today, in that impossibly yellow car. That was at least something.

"Hey." It's Manny. He must have come from the side entrance, because Stevie's been here at least fifteen minutes, freezing his dick off but unable to move.

"Hey." He's only seen Manny once this past month, when Manny visited him in the hospital. It was a few days after the accident. Stevie'd had to stay a week – for observations, they'd said. Manny stopped in late one night, long after visiting hours. He'd brought a bottle of Jack and sat in the seat near Stevie's bed, not saying anything but repeatedly touching the cut on his head where they'd stitched him up, like maybe he expected to still feel blood. Finally, he asked if Stevie remembered anything. Stevie shook his head. He could not bear to tell his friend that he remembered everything. That he recalled soaring through the air, hurling away from the sounds of crunching metal and the smell of burning rubber. That he was suspended on cottony clouds as the car flipped once, then twice, then maybe a third time, rolling and rolling some more – away from him. That he saw the flames fly up and punch the sky just as he met his Great Grandpa Gus somewhere around the roiling seas of Cape Horn. That he heard the stereo still playing from his dream—cushion until finally those moments passed and all went silent. And that he knew in the moment he hit the frozen cornfield that he was not dead but that someone surely was. How could they not be? No, he did not tell Manny all that. He just shook his head and took the bottle of Jack.

Now they're both standing here on the steps of Our Lady of Sorrows. The whole community's here. Half the school, too. Stevie did not expect to see Manny, but he's glad he's here, even if he doesn't know what to say. He wishes Manny'd just pass a bottle.

Two women come up the steps. The doorway is small and the boys have to turn sideways as the women slide past. "Should have a fuckin' program or something," says Stevie. "You know – to hand out." As soon as he says it, he's sorry. Like there's a program for how this all goes. Like a program will change the stabbing pain they've lived with for a month and the quiet whispers filling the air today. He knows there are programs inside that will walk them all through the next hour but will fail to tell them anything they need to know. He knows the program will mark this day forever, Thursday, February 13, in the year of Our Lord 2014. One month to the day after the crash. He wishes to God he hadn't said that thing about the program because now he worries Manny thinks he's supposed to say something back. He knows Manny's got nothing to say. He knows all eyes are secretly on Manny and Manny's not supposed to be here. He knows Manny's not in the program.

It's cold but Stevie is suddenly sweating. He's not ready for this. How could he be? How could any of them be?

Rick's nowhere to be seen. Stevie's glad because he doesn't want to talk to him, not here, not now. He wishes he were here so Manny would have someone else to talk to. He sees Rick in Trig class every day, but he can't talk to him today.

Who he really wants to talk to is Lucky. Lucky'd know what to say. He'd smile that stupid crooked smile, pass a joint – yeah, even here – and say, *Go on, pussies, get on with it.* He'd laugh at them for being such dicklesses. He'd laugh at them for wearing pressed shirts. He'd stroll out to the lemon–yellow Kia and open the door and pull out a whole box of tissues and wipe his girl's snotty nose and turn around and smile his stupid crooked grin. He'd see all the dopey people and say *Fuck this* and hijack the Kia and drive off into a yellowy cottony haze. He'd say *What're you waitin' for?* so Manny and Stevie would hop in the back seat and they'd drive to the South River where Lucky'd climb out of the car and strip down to his Jockeys and jump – *Geronimo!* – into the freezing river, just to show them he had more balls than any of them, and come up spluttering *Fuuuuuck* and grinning again, all goosebumpy and shrivelled. He'd sit in the car drying out with the heat and stereo blasting and tell them all they're losers for not jumping in, too. He'd look back at Manny and Stevie, wonder why he's driving and not Manny, wonder for a moment why they are in Ellie's mom's car but then shrug and glance around again, saying, "Hey, where's Rick?"

He'd do all those things, and more. He'd graduate next year and go to University of Maryland, get a degree in biology and eventually become a high school teacher and soccer coach. He'd still light up with Stevie and the boys – they'd pass a bottle of Jack around on a Thursday night after poker, get a little stoned, and reminisce about what bad–asses they were back in the day. He'd be a great soccer coach – he already coaches the Brave Bears in town, because no one else will. He's a stoner, sure, but he's a stoner who can outrun anyone on the soccer field and average two goals a game all season. He's actually quite something, Lucky is.

"Have you been inside?" asks Stevie.

"Yeah," says Manny.

There is a long pause until Manny finally says, "He's all laid out neat. Dressed in a suit like a pussy."

Stevie sees Ellie pull down the visor and put on lipstick. He knows he should go to her and help her out of the car, help her take that first step. He knows her mother is nowhere to be found, and he feels deep in his gut that no one should have to emerge from that impossibly fucked up cheerful yellow car and step toward the darkness inside.

A celebration of life, it will say on the program.

Yeah. Fuck.

He moves to go down the steps when Manny reaches out and grabs his forearm. He thinks Manny's going to say something but instead a sob breaks forth from a place he's never seen or heard before. Manny says loudly, "Fuckin' Lucky ... he was supposed to live! He was supposed to ... *wake up!*" Stevie is aware of all eyes on them, here on the threshold of Our Lady of Sorrows. "He was supposed to wake up, man!" Manny says again.

Stevie feels the weight of Manny collapse onto him. He's holding him and shivering. He puts both arms around his bulky frame and realises that no one has done this in a month for Manny. No one. He feels the weight of metal and fire and rubber and burning hell in Manny's heaving shoulders. He holds his friend.

He sees Ellie open the door of her mother's yellow Kia and step out. There's a snotty wadded tissue in her hand and she walks toward them, alone.

Friday, 14th February 2014

The Thaw

by Len Kuntz

On the second Friday in February, a raucous thaw begins. Ruptures of ice, one after the other, crack like cannons, echoing in the snow—encrusted treetops. The lake is no better than a defenseless animal under attack, as slabs explode and drop into her dark belly.

Rosie ambles into the kitchen, nosing my hand to be petted, and behind her, Virginia, the woman whose home I've been staying at the last month.

"Sounds like torpedoes," she says. "I'll bet it's something to see."

Virginia taps the edge of the counter, feeling her way toward the coffee pot, retrieving a cup from the cupboard, and filling it precisely to the brim.

"What's it look like out there?"

"Destruction," I say, "but kind of beautiful, in an angry sort of way."

"Beautiful and angry. How wonderful. More coffee?" she asks holding up the pot.

"I'm good."

The night I arrived at Virginia's house, after a five hour trek across the frozen lake, she answered her door and welcomed me in without any hesitation, as if I was a relative instead of a complete stranger. Later I learned that she was widowed, childless and lonely. I hadn't expected to stay this long, but fell into a comfortable pattern of laziness. Other than once on the phone with my wife, I haven't spoken to anyone but Virginia and her Labrador, Rosie.

"Now that the weather's turning, I suppose you'll be going soon," Virginia says. Her housecoat has flapped open and I can see the gleaming outline of one of her bare breasts. She's just past sixty, yet fit for her age, hardly wrinkled except for a smattering of crow's feet. Despite her being blind, I feel sleazy for staring and take Rosie's snout in my hands.

"Yeah. Maybe this afternoon."

When I told my wife I wasn't at our house, she said good, because she'd moved in with her boss. She said I should be on the lookout for divorce papers in the mail. She said marrying me was the worst thing that's ever happened in her life, which is some kind of dagger considering she was sexually assaulted by her father for years as a child.

As if channeling my thoughts, Virginia says, "So your marriage, it's over then?"

I remember the few nights we made love, when my wife's fingernails pierced the skin of my neck, nothing kinky or erotic about it, just her disdain of me being verified.

"Over and done," I say, realizing for once what a release it is to be finally free.

"Relationships are quite a challenge."

"But you were married for thirty years."

"Yes, and most of the time I was miserable. If David hadn't died, I think I would have ended up killing him."

"Why stay then, in a bad marriage?"

Virginia points to her eyes, wide as they always are. "I'm pretty independent, but being blind is a tricky thing to negotiate all alone."

I stayed in my marriage because my identity was all wrapped up in being Jess's husband, her a successful bond broker, me a failed alcoholic.

"Would you happen to have a drink handy?" I ask.

"Water?"

"Something harder."

Virginia's eyebrows arch. She likes the idea. "Well, why not, it's noon somewhere. There are a few bottles in the shelf above the fridge."

I haven't had a drop of alcohol in five years, not since the car accident, then losing my job and not having the confidence or wherewithal to get a new one. I thought that being sober would center me, that I'd discover my true, authentic self as they say in AA, but I only felt more lost, empty and soulless.

I make us screwdrivers, mine mostly vodka. The first taste is like seeing old yearbook photos. I don't know what I'm doing, but I'm enjoying the missile of heat that slakes along my nerves, making my senses electric. I have another and another. As if I'm leafing through a magazine, I start to count my past mishaps and failures, picturing them in my mind, bloody and glossy.

I don't even realize that Virginia has gotten up and is standing behind me until I feel her hands on my shoulders. "You've gotten quiet all of a sudden."

When she leans forward, her breasts are squeezed over my head like earmuffs, warm and plush.

She whispers in my ear, "Before you go, do you think you could do me a favor?"

Rosie's asleep on her mat. My glass is empty. Outside the ice sounds like steel beams breaking.

"It's been a very, very long time for me," Virginia says, kissing my head. "And after all, it is Valentine's Day."

I put my hands over hers, ready to push them off. Instead I grip Virginia's fingers, stand and walk with her toward the bedroom.

Saturday, 15th February 2014

Second Inning

by Michael Webb

I see her as I enter the clubhouse. Spring training is now big business, even during the pitchers and catchers portion, so it doesn't surprise me to see press on hand. She's wearing a thin, gauzy, lime–colored dress, appropriate in the Florida heat, but too thin for the chill of the locker room. She walks towards me, smiling.

"Mark Hamilton?" she says cheerfully.

"Y—yes," I say. "I didn't expect to be recognized so soon."

"Hi! I'm Jen from Comcast. I covered you in Chicago. Well, I was an intern then. But I was there." I think about that year in Chicago for a moment, the long climb into the playoffs, followed by the abrupt exit.

"How about that," seems like the only thing to say. There are a few other pitchers and clubhouse attendants scattered around the room, everyone suddenly intent on their shoes.

"It's so nice to see a familiar face," she says. She focuses on me, her television eyes wide and fluttering. "I have to come up with six items for the website every day," she continues, "and I just don't know how I'm going to do that."

"I'm sure you'll manage," I say.

"You were always such a gentleman then," she says, standing a bit closer. "Do you think you can give me a hand with that?"

"Well," I say. "You were in Chicago, you've been around the game. You know the drill."

"It's just that I don't know any of these guys much. Would you mind if I come to you for quotes when I'm stuck?"

"Of course," I say. "As long as you don't mind the usual predigested crap."

She smiles, a brilliant sunrise that shows why she has a job on television. "Oh, I don't think they even care. As long as I fill space."

"Well, I can fulfill your BS quota, for sure. I've played long enough, I know all the clichés. You've probably heard them all, too."

"Oh yes," she says, chuckling, tucking a long strand of hair back into place. "I could probably write them without you. You just want to fit in, do your job, and as long as you execute, you'll help put the team in position to win. All that 'one game at a time' stuff Kevin Costner says on the bus in *Bull Durham*."

I smile back. "That's it, exactly."

"Seriously, though. Can I count on you?" She shifts her weight from hip to hip, pulling her dress tight across her taut abdomen.

"Sure," I say. "I'm not going to rat anyone out. But I'll help you fill space. That's no problem."

"Thanks," she says. "They want you to do everything now. Radio, web, TV, podcast. Plus all new content for every platform. It is such a strain. And like I said, I don't know anybody here yet. Plus you're not like some of these idiots." She looks down at her toes, brilliant and scarlet against the red and gray carpet.

"Well, just ask my wife about that."

She laughs. "No, no. I mean, some of the players, you know."

"Animals? Well, you know I'm not like that."

"Yeah," she says. "That's why I appreciate it so much. It's nice to have a friend. I'm new in town too."

A notion trickles up from my subconscious. "Hey, do you think maybe …" I begin.

I hear the sound of footsteps in the tunnel, followed by John "Tex" Holman, the multimillionaire kid closer consuming most of the attention and oxygen in the few days the team has spent together so far, all spiked hair and braggadocio. A print reporter with a beard follows along beside him, nodding and smiling like a courtier to a prince. In an instant, my new friend turns, walking towards the tumult. I watch her walk, suddenly hip− twitchingly alluring and seductive.

"Hey, Tex!" she says as she walks, her voice an octave higher, leaving me to bend low and untie my shoes.

A Visit from Mother

by James Claffey

Over the river the Bird pedals, the brittle sound of rubber on macadam as he makes his way home. The beam from his lamp yellows a narrow strip ahead of the bicycle, the rainclouds blocking out the moonlight. In the fields on either side of the road plastic—covered hayrolls stand as silent monuments, the only sound the rain pattering on plastic. Far to the right the Bird eyes the humped mound of the fairy fort.

As a boy his classmates once tied him with rope and left him there on a dark Halloween night. By the time the Bird extricated himself from the knots, the screech owls were calling to one another, and muffled drumbeats seeped from beneath the ground. He ran home in tears, the jeers and cruelty of his classmates stored in his memory for another day.

He thumbs the Rosary ring on his right hand, repeating the Hail Mary's and Our Father's falling behind him on the road as he pedals townwards. On the final downhill approach to town he sings the Hail Holy Queen in full voice as he freewheels across the bridge to the corner, where he dismounts, blesses himself, and unfastens his pants' legs from the bicycle clips. He could, he knows, cycle the route blindfold, the number of times he's traveled that road in the past, but if a squirrel, or a cat, or dog crossed his path, he'd be smashed to bits if he crashed.

In the house all is quiet and he moseys about the kitchen for a bit of supper. He puts a match to the cooker and sets the kettle on the hob. Bread and cheese, both a bit hardened about the edges, but beggars can't be choosers, he thinks as he spreads a pat of yellow butter on the loaf. In the mirror above the dresser he catches sight of his reflection and even though he's not the handsomest of men, he at least has all his hair, not like that hoor, Maurice McGettigan, bald as the Dome of St. Peter's. Swarthy, too. Might be black Irish, a touch of the Spaniard about him, by all accounts. Didn't someone tell him Maurice slept well past midday most mornings? Siesta, they call it over there, he thinks. Bloody laziness, more like.

The Bird wedges a bit of bread and cheese in his mouth and chews diligently until the kettle whistles and he fills the teapot to the brim. After commiserating with himself over the French girl's not showing up at the Sunday *seisiun*, he distracts himself with a look at the Sunday crossword puzzle. He licks the tip of the pencil, tasting the familiar lead flavor, the same taste from all those years ago at the local secondary school. Back then the inkwells in the desks were little ceramic pots, and the students would spend hours soaking spitballs in ink and flicking them at one another with their rulers and setsquares.

After flicking the light switch off, the Bird mounts the stairs and in his bedroom undresses and lies on top of the sheets naked. He thinks of the beautiful Melodie, her smile, the twinkle in her eye as she played the reels. Charm, that's what she has, he decides. And the next time he sees her, well, he's going to go through his mammy's necklaces and pick out the finest one to present her with. Ladies like jewelry, that's what his daddy had told him often. Treat them like precious stones, and you'll be all right, he'd told his son. The Bird wonders if his daddy ever listened to his own advice. Many's the time he'd arrive home from school to the pair of them going at it hammer and tongs.

He stares at the picture of Christ on the wall. The Sacred Heart of Jesus, indeed. He should have taken it off the wall when the pair of them had died, but instead he'd transplanted it from their bedroom wall to where it now hangs. He shifts positions so he can avoid Jesus's eyes searching his face and soon is asleep on top of the covers. When he wakes, it's to a loud thump nearby and an odd moaning sound. Chilled from the night air, his arms and legs are covered in goose bumps, so he pulls trousers and shirt on and takes the small statue of St. Anthony by the head for protection.

The landing is in darkness and only the moonlight coming through the window allows the Bird to find his way without stumbling. He grips the doorknob to his parents' bedroom in his free hand and turns the knob. Inside, the room is quiet, but a rocking noise comes from the wardrobe.

"Come out, you hoor!" he shouts, raising St. Anthony above his head, ready to crown whoever's in the wardrobe. The door rattles. The Bird takes a step backward. The door creaks and his ginger−haired mother opens the closet door, wearing a knit wool cap and a pair of angel wings. As she holds both arms out as if to cradle her son, he crawls up against the bedstead and forces himself not to look at her naked, fat body. It's one thing to behold your own mother in "that" way, but to see her appear out of your own closet, clad in a wool beanie, all done up like a seagull gone awry, is too much to bear. "Oh dear Jesus," the Bird exclaims when she hops on the end of the bed and jumps up and down as if the mattress were her own personal trampoline. "Go away. You're only a figment of my poor imagination, aren't you?" A cloud of lint and dust rises from the bed and he begs her again, "Arrah, would you let me alone, Mammy. Isn't enough you tortured me when you were alive."

"Puritan," she hisses, flapping the angel wings and stirring up more lint, or perhaps dust from the wings. "You'll have to make me go away," she says.

The Bird slides off the bed and swings the statue of St. Anthony in wide circles. "I'll take the head off you if you don't leave me be." He brings the saint down on the bed with a dull thump and sends his mother fluttering for the lightshade. A wingtip touches the bulb and the smell of burning flares his nostrils. His mother lands by the closet door and when he looks across at her, a strange orange glow fills the inside of the closet, and with one hop, his mother disappears into the floorboards.

"Jesus Mary and Joseph," he says, searching the wardrobe for signs of his mother's ghost, or whatever he just witnessed, "I'll give up the drop for a year if you never darken my doorstep." The silence in the room is too much for him to bear, and he returns the statue to the other room, goes over to the small, walnut bedside table and turns the transistor to Radio 2. A loathsome punk band, the Radiators from Space, is playing and in disgust he presses the off button.

Under the covers, he fidgets and turns, sleep refusing his call. The creak of a floorboard has him on his feet, gravitating towards the statue once more. When he treads on the landing carpet the creak sounds again and he tiptoes towards the staircase. Down to the hall he goes, statue gripped in both hands as if it'll protect him from whatever apparition he might encounter.

The house is empty and he drags a chair out from the kitchen table and sits in the center of the room until the day lightens outside and the first birdsong comes. He thinks of his mother, his dear old mother, transformed into some hideous winged creature, and the tears run down his cheeks. At this moment he understands the house is no better than a tomb, and he might as well have been buried alive when his parents died.

Live For

by Gwendolyn Joyce Mintz

They've agreed to meet. Same place, same time, but Mora and Diane get to Kelly's Bar & Grill late. They follow the hostess to the booth where Aaron waits for them.

He is not alone.

Mora gives a quick once−over to the two men sitting to Aaron's left. One is early twenties, she figures. Wears thick−lensed glasses and has a scruffy mop of brown hair on his head as well as face and chin.

The other is older, late twenties, she's sure. She can't get a good look at him because he's staring into the near−empty drink in his hand. Mora notes, however, that he is beginning to lose his hair on top.

Aaron smiles at the young women. "Hail, hail," he says, "the gang is finally all here."

Mora lifts a brow.

The scruffy guy moves in, toward Aaron, but the other guy stands.

"I like the end," he tells Diane.

Mora peels her coat off before easing into the curved wooden seating next to Aaron. Giving him a brief hug, she whispers, "Why are you wearing glasses, who are these people and are you drunk?"

Aaron touches the rim of the black metal–framed glasses and grins. "I slept in my contacts, eyes are a mess." He picks up the beer bottle before him and brings it to his lips. After a drink, he points the bottle at the man sitting next to him. "This is Phil and that guy," he adds, shifting the bottle to the man next to Diane, "is Vincent. I met them on an internet forum."

"On dying," Phil says.

"But they have been cleared for membership," Aaron declares, setting the beer bottle down with a slight thud. "You wanna die, this is the place to be."

"Vincent," Diane says. "Kind of apropos." She unbuttons her jacket and shrugs it off.

"What is?" Mora asks.

Running her fingers down her hair falling on both sides of her face, Diane hooks the blonde strands behind her ears. "That song," she replies. "The one about van Gogh."

"Hmm," Aaron murmurs. He hums a few bars of *Vincent (Starry, Starry Night)*. "This is to those with no hope inside," he says. He raises the bottle in the air for a moment then presses it to his lips, finishing the beer off. Placing it on the table, he leans toward Mora and whispers, "And, yes, I am drunk."

She glares.

"What?" he asks.

"You tell me," she replies.

The server arrives with the water for Mora and Diane and to take their drink order. Diane wants a margarita on the rocks. Mora simply shakes her head 'no.'

When the server leaves, Aaron tells Mora. "We ordered nachos."

Mora raises her brow and exhales. She looks across the table and wonders why Phil's left hand remains out of sight.

Aaron addresses Phil and Vincent. "As president de facto of The Suicide Club, I invite you to fully introduce yourself and your story, while I get another beer." He waves down their server – Lindsey – as she is leaving a nearby table.

"Something else?" she asks.

"You don't need another drink," Mora tells Aaron.

"Since you are *not* my girlfriend, you don't get to tell me what I need."

His words, the bitter and sharp tone, smack her head back in surprise.

Aaron's apology is immediate. "I'm drunk," he says.

"Given that confession, I'll bring you water," the server tells Aaron. She scoops up the beer bottle as well as Vincent's glass, and departs.

Diane stares across the table at Mora, who's looking back at her.

What the hell? Mora mouths.

Vincent is sifting through the near—empty bowl of popcorn. He picks out the last few popped kernels, tosses them into his mouth.

Aaron leans his head back and watches the ceiling.

Phil says, "This is an interesting idea." With his right hand, he adjusts his glasses.

Mora wonders how many times as a child he heard the words: "coke bottles."

Diane turns to him. "The club?"

He nods. "On the forum, when people talk about committing suicide, others try and talk 'em out of it."

Vincent grunts. "Or they ask why you're on the computer and not doing the deed."

A smile comes to Aaron's face as he lowers his head and faces the group. "They like doers not talkers."

"But we're gonna talk *in order to do*, right? I mean, the point to this is to support each other so that we do kill ourselves," Diane says.

"Why would you want to kill yourself – you're so pretty."

Diane shakes her head. She lifts the glass of water to her lips and drinks 'til it's empty. She sets the glass on the table and spins it with her two hands.

"Pretty people kill themselves all the time. Models. Actresses," Mora tells Phil, in answer to his comment. "She's not looking for a why; we're here for the how and when." She leans back, crosses her arms in front of her. Then she says, "Let's go get a cigarette." An invitation meant only for Diane.

She nods. Scoops up her jacket and they leave.

"You said they were cool."

Aaron assures Vincent they – Mora and Diane – are. "We're just off tonight." He sighs. "This is a bust."

Phil and Vincent agree.

It takes Mora more than one try to get the cigarette lit.

Diane paces before her. "Aaron's weird tonight."

Mora nods as she takes a long drag. Though she doesn't tell Diane, she knows that he drinks to excess only when he's emotionally hurting.

"And those guys he brought with him."

"Why would you want to kill yourself – you're so pretty," Mora mimics.

Diane grins. "Maybe he thinks only ugly people should die."

Mora grunts. "What does that say about his self–image?"

Diane shakes her head at her friend's comment. "That is so wrong."

Mora shrugs and finishes her cigarette.

"We staying?" Diane asks.

Mora's curls tremble as she shakes her head in haste. "I say we blow this joint."

When the women return, Aaron says, "We're gonna call this."

"Not a problem," Mora replies. She scoops up some cheese–covered tortilla chips from the plate.

"I want my drink," Diane says, picking up the glass that has come, along with the nachos, in her absence. She stands, sipping at it.

Vince and Aaron scoot out of the booth.

Phil's left hand is on the table.

Mora notes a deformity as he moves to get up as well. She wonders about his story but is in no mood to stay and find out.

Aaron pulls out his wallet and throws some bills on the table. "This is on me."

"Give me your keys, Aaron."

"What?"

"Keys." Mora holds her hand up and flicks her wrist as if she were working the ignition.

Aaron stares at her for a moment then he drops them in her upturned hand.

"I'll let you kill yourself," she tells him, "but you're not bringing anyone on the road into this."

They don't talk on the drive to Aaron's apartment. But there, he and Mora sit outside on the step by the front door, waiting for Diane, who was following them, to arrive.

Though Mora has mittens, her arms wrapped tight around her body and her pink knit scarf coiled around her neck, Aaron can feel her shivering.

"If you're too cold, we can go inside."

"Nope." She folds at the waist, crosses her arms on her knees and lays her head down. "What was your problem tonight?"

"You."

Mora springs up. "What?"

Aaron doesn't turn from her questioning and accusing stare. "Friday was the 14th. It was very unlucky for me."

"What?" Mora tilts her head. "I didn't know you were superstitious; but it's the 13th that isn't lucky. Last Friday was —" Her eyes widen.

"Yeah, Valentine's Day. And I wanted to spend it with you."

Mora turns away. She sighs a heavy breath.

"That was on my list of things I wanted to do before I died. I like you, Mora. I always have."

"Diane should show up right now. As if on cue."

"Please," Aaron reaches out for her hand. "Just listen to me."

Mora nods.

Aaron opens his mouth but says nothing. He starts again then shakes his head.

"We tried already; we don't work, remember?"

Aaron nods. "I just wanted to be with you." He turns his attention to the road. "You wouldn't stay the night."

Her answer is immediate. "No." Still Mora leans toward him. When he faces her again, she presses her mouth against his. After a minute or so, she pulls away slightly, and tells him, "Don't say something dumb or corny like that was to die for."

Aaron shakes his head. He promises not to.

Diane arrives.

Aaron pulls Mora to him, buries his face in the nest of her dark curls.

"I have to go," she whispers.

He nods. Releasing her, watching her trot down the walk to the car, he wants to tell her if he didn't have other plans, it — she — would certainly be something to live for.

Living Dead

by Stephen V. Ramey

Doctor D is a fortyish woman with short, dark hair and wide hips. She doesn't smile often, but she's pleasant enough. I see her for a checkup every couple years, and then we part ways. It's like the mating ritual of a nomadic cat, or *Star Trek* Spock. Yes, I know that show. That's where I learned that people have specific roles, and the captain always gets the girl.

I never wanted to "get the girl". I wanted to find someone who would love me for me, hold their own in discussions of right and wrong, and inspire me to become a better man. Anne was that person, and she found me. It was a story about lima beans and self–hatred that did the trick. "I glimpsed your soul in that story," she told me years later. "I knew you were the one."

The door swings open, and in steps Dr. D. I like the way her eyes flare at first contact. It's like watching an ember settle. Her real name is D'Onosto or something. A young man trails her. He's wearing scrubs like the nurse who took my vitals earlier.

"Scott will be assisting today," Dr. D says. I nod to him, and he sort–of–nods back. He must be new.

"How have you been feeling?" Dr. D says. She takes my hands and moves the joints around.

"No complaints," I say.

We go through the ritual, Dr. D methodically probing glands, thumping knees, listening to my heart and lungs.

"How are you tolerating the cholesterol pills?" she says.

"I quit taking them. Free samples are fine – thanks for that – but I can't afford a hundred bucks a month."

She frowns like a concerned mother. "You can't just go on and off those pills, Stephen. There are risks."

"Anne has me on Niacin," I say.

"Make sure it's time–release." Dr. D glances at a chart. "Your blood pressure was one–thirty over ninety. That's borderline high." She scribbles something. "I'm going to have Scott draw blood. I want to check for sugar since your father had diabetes, and cholesterol, of course. And I want to do a PSA to establish a baseline for you." She nods to Scott. Hands trembling ever so slightly, he tourniquets my upper arm and arranges vials as if he's familiar with the process. I look away. It hurts worse if I watch the needle go in.

A pinch. I wince, and look back as blood surges into the first vial. I feel a splash of guilt. Why is my blood so anxious to escape? Scott rotates to a second vial, then a third. He caps and labels the samples while Dr. D pulls on rubber gloves.

"I need to examine your testicles," she says.

Oh God, I think, *I forgot this part.* With stoic precision, I hop down from the table and unbutton my fly. Pants accordion down to my knees. I pull down my briefs.

Dr. D squats. I feel embarrassed. What about all that hair, the gray and the brown and the messy tufts? *Pubic defoliation, pro or con?* I think. The practiced intensity of Dr. D's expression stops me asking her. She doesn't enjoy this either. *Let it go.*

She squeezes my balls, slides my foreskin up and back, and stands. We do not make eye contact.

I reach to pull up my pants.

"One more thing." She lubricates her gloved finger.

"Do we have to?"

"No," Dr. D says. "But we should. I need to see if your prostrate is enlarged. You're of an age, as they say."

"I'm not having problems," I say. *Other than the sudden urges to pee, difficulty initiating a stream. And my erections leave a lot to be desired.*

"Lean onto the table," she says. "I'll be quick."

My eyes seek out Scott, but he's having none of it. *You're on your own, dude.*

I wince as Dr. D wriggles her finger up my butt. I feel cold all over. Memory flashes of Rose lifting my hand to her cheek. It's ludicrous. This is not even remotely the same.

Anne and I walk downtown for a late lunch to celebrate my checkup. She's always on the lookout for opportunities to reward good behavior. That I didn't find an excuse to duck out of the physical she scheduled for me months ago, qualifies.

The day is cold, but sunny. I haven't worn gloves, and my coat is only partway zipped. *Winter's losing its grip*, I hope.

"How's The Fountain sound?" Anne says as we stroll the northeast facet of The Diamond. The Diamond is a roundabout, only the lanes form angles rather than a circle, and it's bisected by the busiest highway in town. The effect is of triangular islands divided by a short stretch of highway with stop−lighted intersections. A statue depicts a Civil War soldier on one side of Highway 18, a fountain burbles on the other.

We cross the street to a hole−in−the wall cafe with a drooping, rusted awning and battered sign. The Fountain is a mainstay in New Castle, but has fallen out of favor in recent years (decades?). When we first moved here, I poked around on Google, and found this review: *Pleasant little place to sit and work quietly or relax over a cup o' joe. Betty the waitress is still here after 61 years of "how ya doin', honey" hospitality.*

And that is exactly right.

Bells jingle as I swing the door open. I smell grilled lamb. The dining area is deceptively deep, as are all the stores in these old buildings. A lunch counter stretches along one wall, fronting a polished soda fountain. Vintage signs hang everywhere: *Coca-Cola, Orange Fezz, Barq's*. Through a serving window at the back, I see the owner, a seventy-something Greek man, perched on a stool overlooking the grill. He's reading a newspaper.

Anne and I slide into opposite sides of a booth. The springs are shot, and duct tape covers several tears in the green vinyl. Still, there's a cozy comfort here, the sense of visiting a more innocent time.

Betty brings laminated menus. "Hi, honey, how're you doing today?"

"Fine," Anne and I say together. At 84 years young, and with her hair piled high, Betty reminds me of the Bride of Frankenstein, in a good way. Hers is the human face, the gentleness that Frankenstein's monster could never master.

"What can I get yinz to drink?" she says with a friendly smile. I think of Anne's father taking out his bridge because it doesn't fit his mouth.

My order for *Coke* gets translated to *Pepsi*, then, "Sorry, hun, I just sold the last one. Is diet okay?"

Anne orders iced tea, and Betty shuffles off. I watch her lug a pitcher to a group of white-mustachioed men at a table in the back. One man laughs, and the grating sound bounces around the room until it is exhausted of emotion. For an instant, I'm in a Hollywood scene, a dusty restaurant inhabited by the living dead. Nostalgia crumbles. The Fountain is not so much a pleasant reliving of the past, as a pointless denial of the truth that all things die.

My phone buzzes, and I startle. Anne looks over the edge of her menu. There's a list of daily specials pinned to the front. I can't remember what day it is.

Another buzz. I take the phone from my pocket. It's Doctor D's office. Panic flutters and subsides.

"I better take this outside," I say. Reception is spotty in these brick buildings. "Order my usual."

Anne frowns. "You don't have a usual. We've only eaten here a couple times."

"Then order whatever you think *should* be my usual." I slide from the booth and hurry outside, phone pressed to my ear.

"Yes?"

"Stephen? This is Doctor D'Orenzio. I have the results from your blood work. A couple of things concern me."

"Oh?" Cold sweeps into me. I zip my coat.

"I felt a couple nodes in your prostate," she says, "and your PSA is 8.5."

"Is that bad?"

"It's not good." She sighs. "It may be nothing, Stephen, I don't mean to worry you. But I want you to see a specialist."

How much is this going to cost? is my first thought, not, *OMG, Cancer!*

"I can recommend several good people," Doctor D says. "That's one benefit of living in a geriatric city."

I can't help seeing my father in his final days, blood splattering from his lips, that horrid grasping fear in his eyes. I can't help seeing myself in that bed, Anne at my side. She looks determined. She looks sad.

I'm the reason you're destitute, I think. *I'm the reason you could never be content.*

"No," I hear as if from a distance, then firmer, "No."

"What do you mean?" Dr. D says.

"No specialist," I say. I snap the phone shut before she can continue. *This is where it ends*, I think. *This is where I die.* The idea is not as frightening as I want it to be.

Nesting

by Gay Degani

A warm February morning, Sybil on her porch, wearing one of the silk robes she ordered from the internet. She sips sugared coffee and studies her bunions, her swollen ankles, the varicose veins tracing up her calves, all the while keeping an ear out for the blue jay. She's filled the crystal candy bowl on the table next to her with sunflower seeds, a peanut or two. It's been a month now since wind stormed the Old Road at 90 mph, knocking down trees, severing electrical wires, turning the neighborhood into a disaster area, a month since Jamie and the kids climbed into their dilapidated old car and disappeared, a month since Sybil last saw the jay.

Most of her property, the group of five small rental houses facing a courtyard, has been cleaned up by tenants pitching in with rakes and wheelbarrows, but the front bungalow where Jamie lived is still buried beneath thick heavy limbs and red–tagged as uninhabitable. As for the blue jay, with his smart–aleck chirp and curious nature, he too lost his nest when the giant oak tumbled.

"Morning, Beautiful," Ian calls from the porch of bungalow #2. He's the newest resident in Sybil's domain, a thirty–two–year–old man whose mother, a real estate agent, employs him to sit on her open houses, hire cheap labor to "polish" her listings, and flirt with female clients. She also pays his rent, one of the many parental "trends" that causes Sybil to wonder what the world is coming to.

"You're up early," she says. "Want some coffee?"

"I'd love some." He's already striding over on long legs, his lanky body awkward in a dark blue suit, light blue shirt, pink tie, his eyes cobalt, his grin charming. "Any word from your insurance company yet?"

Sybil grabs a paper napkin and dusts off the other rattan chair. "They're taking care of it, though I haven't seen any money yet."

"They've set up a loan center somewhere over at city hall for storm damage. Dress in that hot yellow dress of yours and they'll whip out their checkbooks."

"I've owned this place free and clear for forty years, Ian Shane, and I'm not about to go into debt now. Let me get you that coffee." She heads inside, thinking, why'd I invite him over? She never did learn to keep her distance from tenants. You'd think by now. Probably the blue suit. She's missing the jay. That's it, but talking to the bird is a lot more fun than talking to Ian Shane.

She returns with a small thermal pot, another cup, and a plate of chocolate biscotti on a tray, and the man's face lights up. He thinks he's got her now.

"You know, Sybil, you're sitting on a gold mine here."

"You want to start digging?"

"Funny, but I'm serious. Don't you want to be done with this headache?" He gestures at the property, the fallen tree sprawled across the front bungalow, the stop sign on the corner bent like a flex straw, the telephone pole braced by 4x8s, not yet replaced. "With all the redevelopment going on around here, I can find you a buyer in no time and put you in a nice condo downtown, one of those penthouse lofts with stainless steel appliances where you wouldn't have to do anything."

"Stainless steel appliances," she says with derision. "You want Splenda or real sugar?"

"Black, thank you. You brew better than Starbucks. Come on, Sybil. Think about it. Walking distance to the movies, restaurants, Target. I know you love Target."

What a con artist! She sips her coffee. Doesn't tell him she's been thinking about selling. Started thinking about it since he first brought it up the day after the windstorm, but she's owned the bungalows on the Old Road since 1971 when her grandfather passed away and she moved in, letting that grease monkey "what's—his—name" come with her. Memories should be enough to keep her here, the lovers who paraded in and out of her little house over the years, the tenants who brought her turkeys for Christmas, champagne at New Years, took her to lunch on her birthday, but it's Jamie, she admits now, packing up her kids and taking off without so much as a good—bye, that gives her pause. If she left, she wouldn't be here when they came back. If they come back.

Where had Jamie gone? She missed smart little Lily. The boyness of Collin. At least when Jamie's husband knocked on Sybil's door the day after the storm, she could answer honestly that she didn't know where they were. Had he found her? Sybil didn't even know whether or not Jamie wanted to be found. Jamie'd never confided in her. Never said if Sean was abusive. Sybil didn't think he was, at least not physically. He was selfish, thoughtless, maybe even dishonest, and it seemed that Jamie had simply had enough because she took off without anything. When Sybil and the tenants did the initial clean—up, they'd found her packed suitcase crushed under the tree.

Ian's still talking. "Sybil?"

"Sorry. What'd you say?"

"There's a great place over on Central. Nice view. I could pick up the keys and take you over this morning if you want. Pool, clubhouse, exercise room. Keep that great shape of yours."

"Do you even have your license yet?" She catches him glancing at her neck. Thinks, he's wondering how long I've got before I keel over.

"You want to get out in front of this, Syb."

Syb? *Really?*

"Once everyone on the Old Road decides to sell, you won't get as good a price. My mother says your neighbors are listing their house."

"Which one?" It's her turn to stare, bits of cookie in the corners of his mouth.

"The Treacher mansion next door. They're going to tear it down and put a hotel."

"Never happen."

"They want to bring tourists into the neighborhood like the old days. Put in some cute little shops. Revitalize the creek, that sort of thing."

"Sounds like the perfect time to stay put, not sell." She grins hard, but tugs the two sides of her robe together at the neck, as if clouds have hidden the morning sun. "Aren't you going to be late for work?"

He shrugs. Stretches his legs, sticking his feet between the horizontal bars of the porch railing, his hands behind his head as if he's got nothing better to do than chat up the landlady. Oh right. Today, she thinks, I'm his work. His mother is behind this.

When Ian finally pulls himself to his feet, he thanks her for breakfast and waves good—bye. Adds as he turns the corner toward the carport, "Your blue jay come back yet?"

"No, but he will."

"It's a wild bird. He could be anywhere by now."

"Not so wild, really."

The Follow–Up

by Sally–Anne Macomber

To: Milton Flaxmill, Red Cow Publishing
From: Trudy Polaris
Date: February 20, 2014 10:03 a.m.
Re: Great News

Hi Milton,

Just following up my email from last month, where I sacked you as the publisher of my book *Nuclear Fission in the Pyrénées.* I've thought about it since then and have decided to give you the benefit of the doubt: perhaps the two accents on *Pyrénées* just fell off.

Did you get my email with the explicit instructions for extra spacing for note–makers in the 'academic' edition? If not, I will resend, so please let me know.

I will be offline for a few days as I fly to Europe tomorrow but I will be online again once we settle in to our Tyrolean hideaway.

Glad to have you back on board!

Trudy Polaris

Friday, 21ˢᵗ February 2014

Well, actually

by Mandy Nicol

Celeste watches me fill the dishwasher and I know she's dying to ask me something. Or tell me something. But more likely ask me something. She's driven two hours on a scorcher with a three year–old and Celeste never visits. She prefers to summon. Yes, she must want something all right. So I enjoy myself and place the dishes carefully, with precision, one at a time, even the forks. I think I can hear her teeth grinding.

Mum's in the lounge room reading a dog–eared copy of *Green Eggs and Ham* to her youngest grandchild. The Little Soldier She So Rarely Sees, as she calls him.

I set the dishwasher a–sloshing and sit down at the dining table opposite Celeste. "So what's up?" I ask.

She scowls, "Why should something be up?"

"Okay then, what do you want?"

She smiles, "Well, actually I do have a favour to ask. You know Scott's little sister Angela? She's getting married."

"Oh. That's nice."

"Yes. And I sort of told her that you'd make her dress. I hope you don't mind."

"Why would I mind? It's what I do. I'm hardly going to mind you drumming up business for me. When's the wedding?" Celeste is biting her bottom lip so I add, "And what aren't you telling me?"

'The wedding's in September so you've got oodles of time. Umm, the thing is, I said you'd do it for nothing.'

"Oh. Really?"

Celeste wriggles forward in her seat and plonks her elbows on the table. She is preparing to launch one of her rehearsed and inarguable arguments. I'm too tired so rather than subject myself I say, "Well, I suppose she is family."

Celeste smiles. Cat with the cream and the mouse. "She's hoping you can show her some patterns and samples next weekend," she says.

"That should be okay."

"But you'll have to come to Melbourne because she can't drive."

I scan her face to see if she's joking. She isn't. "Sorry," I say, "That's asking too much."

"Well, actually I told her you would."

"You what?"

"Don't look at me like that, I've thought it all through. You can bring Mum down, drop her off at our place, and pick her up on the way back. It'll only take you an extra twenty minutes or so. And Mum will love it. It will get her out of the house, she'll get to see all the kids, spend some quality time with them." Celeste lowers her voice, "You know how much she misses her grandchildren. It would be a nice thing for you to do for her, Nadia."

Well, actually …

I bite my bottom lip. Hard.

Worry

by Margaret Bingel

Sleep is the brain's way of recharging, and in a coma the patient's mind has an opportunity to dream. At St Jude's Hospital a graduate student monitors a select group's brain waves. She's researching how active the brain is while in a coma versus a vegetative state as part of her thesis, and she had told Nora Billingsly her theory that Nora's son Ned is probably dreaming while in his coma.

"Can he hear?" Nora remembers asking the student.

"Most assuredly," the student had smiled at her. "He can most likely hear everything you say to him. Of course, it's just a theory ..."

Nora can't remember the rest, but she holds on to that theory as she reaches to hold Ned's hand while visiting him at St. Jude's coma ward. Sitting down, she squints at him, squeezing his hand a little, and says, "Morning, Boy."

Nora remembers the phone call she got from the hospital a month ago, the paramedic asking for "Mrs. Billingsly," as if she is married. Only telemarketers ever call her that, and this did not sound like a telemarketer.

"Your son's been in an accident," the paramedic had said. "He's here at St. Jude's."

Time stopped for Nora. My son, she had thought at the time, but that can't be. That won't be him when I get there, she kept thinking while grabbing her coat, walking out the door, leaving her routine of chores and home. It won't be him at all.

She looks into her son's face, and moves her free hand over to his left eye, and opens the eyelid. "Anybody home?" His pupil doesn't dilate. She lets it drop, disappointed. Nora releases her grip on his hand and pulls out a book. She reads to him because she doesn't want him to be bored in his dreams. While she's reading, she's aware of the nurse who comes in to check his vitals, a short, skinny woman who has ashen hair she keeps in one long braid. The nurse marks her clipboard and bustles out of the room, saying nothing.

Nora reads until her throat is dry, and then she knows it's time to leave. She remembers reading somewhere that being close to family helps, but she doesn't know if that's really true. She comes in every Saturday, to read for an hour, but it has been about a month now. How much longer does he need me, she wonders.

Where was I when he needed me to hold his hand?

But her Boy is a Man now, and has been for a while, and he needed to live on his own. She holds her breath, and lets it all out in one, big gust. She lays the bookmark down on the page, and slowly closes the book shut, careful not to crease the pages.

"Goodbye, Boy," she whispers. She rises to her feet, and closing the door behind her, walks out on another Saturday.

Building a Sunday

by Darryl Price

This day, the again of it, that broke my heart with the piano
heavy hammer, that buried me underwater like a bomb from a
different world, another century, that froze the sky in place, solid
like a dream that once was a summer, this day that went up and
up and never came back down, stuck like a fish head between
the avalanche of stars, this day that lost my name forever among
the sad–eyed lint in its pockets, that walked to the edge of the
world without me and fell over into nothing, this day behooves
me, that created a fatal fracture on the surface of the sun on the
bed we shared and seared my skull onto my face like an ancient
bamboo tapped in tattoo, this day you took and hid away from
me in your wisdom, that I'm always looking for in the middle of
the night, this day with its strange overcoat balled up on my sofa,
how can I ever name you properly, how am I supposed to live in
your absence, now that my being is hollow in your shape, now
that my words pour themselves on the floor and must be swept
up and thrown away, now that every object contains the same
emptiness as before, this day that started something but never
finished, this day of ultimate sentencing, this day that disappeared
without warning, that became my ghost, that took the place of
my regular ghost, that appears in the window between a breeze
and some moonlight like someone smoking alone in a cramped
attic, this day that now sits on a shelf like a cat made of rope,

dangling, dangling, waiting for the unseen fire to begin, for the grand awakening of feeling? This awful day. This amazing, dull thing. This precious, lost ball that started it all.

Monday, 24th February 2014

White Rabbit

by Teresa Burns Gunther

Nine days ago

Stella does her business out back then starts digging at the
fence. I poke my head over. The neighbors are making a racket.
Joyce is watering. "What's going on?"

"Oh! Crikey, Rachel!" Joyce says, eyes wide, a hand clapped
to her cavernous cleavage. "You startled me."

"What's all the noise?"

"We're going to raise rabbits!" Joyce says.

"Why?" I envision being overrun, like the Brits. "Will you
eat them?"

She purses her lips. "Well, Larry's talking rubbish about
stew," she says with a jerk of her head at her string bean
husband. "Says, since we can't eat our egg–laying chooks we
may as well eat rabbits for all the money we're spending."

"Sensible," I say. Stella growls. Joyce steps back, wide–eyed,
like Stella will fly over. Joyce is not a dog person.

"Having your coffee?" Larry asks the obvious question and
joins us.

I raise my cup. "Stella heard the noise and woke me," I say,
not to put too fine a point on it.

"Oh, sorry about that. We have to get this finished. We're
going away next weekend – my nephew's graduation." He
beams like it has something to do with him.

Stella barks. She's not crazy about men; who can blame her? Joyce clucks and scurries off, she has it out for my dog.

Two days ago

I'm exhausted from a week of working on my People Skills, #1 of my 2014 Resolutions. My job depends upon it. My face is stiff from smiling. I'd figured I could move on to Resolution #2 – Patience in February, but People Skills are a tough nut to crack.

I refill my coffee and step out on my back porch to enjoy the winter sun on a San Francisco morning. Stella's a blur, shaking something in her mouth, something brown. She's a beauty, a natural hunter, so at first I'm afraid it's Mrs. Franklin's cat. I pull my robe tight and race down my steps, slippery with leftover fog. "Stella, drop it!" She does and looks up, expecting praise for having killed a cat. But it's not a cat. It's a rabbit, stiff, matted and caked with dirt.

"Bad girl, Stella," I say, raising my hand to her. *Hey,* her expression says. *I'll share.* It's a bad habit, raising my hand when I'm upset. I'd never hit her. She's my family now. It's just a reflex I learned from my dad.

I brush the critter off and tell myself *it* snuck into *my* yard. Larry and Joyce's blinds are drawn. Good, still out of town. I don't see the kid who garden–sits, which apparently involves pilfering fruit and smoking dope in their hammock.

I walk the fence and find the hole – big enough for Stella, who sits, poised for play, tail fanning the dirt. "Oh Stella." She cocks her head. I consider sliding the rabbit back through the hole, but they'd know. It wouldn't take much more for Joyce to sick the SPCA on my Stella.

I try to remember when they're coming home. "Come on girl." I wrap the bunny in an old towel, relieved it doesn't stink. I could leave it outside; maybe a hawk would take it. I could tell

104

Joyce I saw it happen, I'm thinking this is brilliant until she wants to know how a hawk got the warren open. I leave it on the washing machine and close the door.

It's still early. Newspapers dot each driveway. I go out for my paper, grab Larry and Joyce's and slip into their side yard. If anyone asks I'm all about "Neighborhood Watch," though I wouldn't be caught dead at the meetings.

I pass their gardening supplies, composting bins – all neat and orderly. I've never accepted an invitation to their parties, so I've never seen the fruits of their noisy labors. Paths wind through flowerbeds filled with citrus and what look like upside down onions, herbs, tipis of fava beans, large leafy kales and colorful chards. I'm in Oz. Bird houses hang throughout the yard; their singing drives my Stella crazy. The *not for eating chooks* are making a ruckus. Fricking Garden of Eden. My yard's a hump of juniper and calla lilies around a concrete slab.

I'm hoping a little face will stare out from the rabbit house, but the door's ajar, the cage empty. I wonder how Stella got it open. She is brilliant!

Fortunately, I'm the only neighbor who can see into their yard. I find the hole. If Joyce found it she'd want Stella's head on a platter.

I find a shovel and refill the hole, a plan forming as I work. I drape an overzealous vine across the dirt and stand back. It looks wild. They'll never know Stella came calling.

Coming out of their yard I bump into the guy three doors down. "Christ!" I say. "You scared the hell out of me." He's decked out in skintight leggings. Nice bod.

He pulls his ear buds out. "What?" He looks from me to Joyce and Larry's house, back to me, confused.

"They're away," I say with a sweep of my hand I slide quick it into my pocket to hide the dirt. "Just taking their papers in."

He smiles.

"Out for your run?" My hand flies up to slap his butt, urge him to get going, until I catch myself and feign a stretch.

"20 miles today," he crows. "Marathon's next week." His smile tells me to be impressed.

"Good for you." I shove my fist in the air. Freak!

"See ya." He waves, sticks his ear—buds in, and sets off.

Stella is howling outside the laundry room when I return. I take the rabbit upstairs, fill the bath and add bubbles. I'm relieved there's no blood. Probably had a heart attack from the shock of Stella's teeth. The bath water turns brown and the rabbit is white. The eyes are filmed over. I can't close them. I dry it with my hair dryer. The fur is so soft. Stella whines at the door.

Not wanting to risk another neighbor run—in, I scramble over the fence and put the rabbit in the cage, on her side, like she's sleeping and close the door. Back on my side I fill what's left of the hole Stella made, press old bricks into the dirt and drag a pot of desiccated geraniums to set on top.

Today

I wake to the smell of coffee I cleverly set the night before. It's not until I step outside for the paper that I remember. Larry stands on the sidewalk cradling his paper, staring into space.

"Oh, hiya Rachel." He's always nice, even though we've had "differences". Joyce is another matter.

"Good trip?"

"Very nice," he says.

"I took your papers around back for you." He doesn't respond. "Everything okay?" My heart's cranking up my heater.

His face creases. "Well, it's weird …"

"Yeah?" My mind races for the explanations I've devised.

"The weirdest thing happened," he said.

"What?" Oh shit.

"We got a rabbit."

"Oh?" I say.

"A little rabbit, Ophelia." He shakes his head.

"What happened?"

"Thing is, she died last week," he said. "We only had her a few days. Joyce was beside herself. Ophelia must have eaten poison in the garden."

"She died?" I asked. "Poison? Isn't that dangerous." I'm pissed and start to say that if Stella had actually eaten it, she'd have been killed but catch myself.

"Yes," he said. "But here's the thing. We buried her before we left, but when I go out this morning —" his eyes go wide, "she's in her cage, just like new."

"Alive?" I ask, hoping for a miracle.

"No." His voice is sad. "I can't make sense of it." He looks back at the house. "Joyce was so upset." His face softens. "The woman has a heart of gold."

I let that slide by. "What did you do?"

"I reburied it. I didn't tell Joyce."

"That's probably wise." I wait for the relief to settle in, but all I feel is deflated.

"Yes. It would freak her out."

I'm surprised to find myself so close, my hand on his shoulder. "Sounds like you did the right thing."

His sorrowful face opens into a snaggle−toothed smile. Then he hugs me! "Thank you, Rachel. You're very kind."

"Me?" It occurs to me to ask to get it in writing, show my boss. But I don't say a word; I have a little lump in my throat.

"Well ... I think that's my phone. Better run."

He's still standing there, smiling at me, the nice Rachel he thinks I am, when I close the door.

Tuesday, 25th February 2014

Morgana Malone and the Case of the Blushing Bride

by Matt Potter

"Oh, God!" Seventeen eyes dart in Zebadie's direction. Looking at me as she lowers her head on the reception desk in exasperation, she breathes out and says, "I soooooo miss porn."

I look over the beige laminate counter into the waiting area. Mr Rubinstein, he of eye no. 17 and an eye patch, bobs up in his chair. I smile and nod, like it's every day the receptionist in a therapy practice admits to working as an adult entertainer in the so—recent past.

"Something caught in her throat," I say, as Mr Rubinstein's eyebrows and eye patch lower. "A bit of déjà vu, I think."

Zebadie – whose neon—blonde like—nylon hair is in thrown—together pigtails today – peers up at me, eyes glistening. "You know what kept me doing porn?" she says. "It wasn't the sex or the practical jokes or the catering, Morgana." And she sniffles at the thought. "It was the conversation. There was always a lot of great conversations happening on the set." A tear appears in the corner of her eye. (Just one.) She sighs, sits up, and reaching under the counter, pulls out a scrapbook with *Wedding Plans* sprayed in Bedazzled jewels on the cover. She opens it and the plastic gems smack the desktop. "That's what first attracted me to Grigor," she says, "his level of conversation. That" – she licks her finger and rifles through to the next page – "and his Porsche."

(It's only my second day here and already I have my favourite patients. "I luff your racink schtripe," Mr Rubinstein said to me earlier, when he walked in, nodding at the grey–brown regrowth yawning through the orange on my head. "They make you go fasta." Smiling under his eyepatch, his toupée undulated on his head like a motley possum caught in the air conditioning draught.)

"The only real downsides to a life in porn are laxatives and plastic surgery," Zebadie says. "And no paid holidays. But it's the kind of job that travels and no one judges you by how fake your orgasms sound because they're all fake. So it's kind of like a level playing field. You store up the real orgasms for the real players. I mean, you have to draw the line *somewhere*."

Zebadie flicks through her wedding planner. She's not really looking at the pages, but sits mesmerized by the colour and movement as each page flicks past at breakneck speed, her wrists working up and down and showing no sign of tiring.

"So I guess porn is paying for your trousseau," I say.

"Well, for my first marriage, it did." And then she touches my forearm with her hand, all blue–eyed wonder. "Don't tell Grigor, though," she whispers. "He still thinks he's the first one."

I look at the push–up bra holding her three and a half boob jobs and the coffee dripolator tan and the scorched hair –

"After my re–birthing," she cuts in, her voice grave and knowing, "of course. Re–birthing means you're also a virgin again." She covers her mouth with her hand, and burps. "Although I want to know if I can get my money back on that one: every morning when I wake up the first thing I smell is placenta. And I don't care what anyone says: that's just not normal."

A door opens and out steps Barry, Grigor's brother and partner in this psychiatry practice, and of course, my ex–

brother—in—law. His hand under her elbow, Barry ushers out an older woman dressed in a black boiler suit, a red pillbox hat perched on her curly grey bob. "Susan will help you with your next appointment," he says.

Boiler suit looks at him, eyebrows quizzical.

"I mean Morgana," Barry says. "Sorry, *Morgana* will help you. *Morgana* will help you with your next appointment."

Sometimes I forget my real name is − was − Susan. And sometimes I forget Barry still calls me the name he first knew me by, when I first met him, when Grigor and I were first married.

Right hand on the mouse as the cursor rolls across the computer screen, I − the new office junior, though I *am* "up−managing" as Grigor told me − focus on looking important: back straight, jaw set, eyes steady.

"Tuesday the 4th at 11.00am," I ask, my eyes on the screen. Though it's not really a question. I type in her name, my hands clunky on the keyboard: *clunk clunk clunk.*

"Tuesday the 4th at 11.00am," Zebadie the office senior (she who's being "up−managed") repeats, large appointment book now open on the desk, her hand curving across the page as she carves the paper with her curly−curly cursive: *scr−a−tch … scr−a−tch … scr−a−tch.*

I click an icon on the screen and a printer spews out a green appointment slip. Reaching across, I tear it off the printer and hand it to boiler suit lady, who slips it inside her boiler suit breast pocket.

I don't know if Tuesday the 4th at 11.00am is good or bad. That's not what I'm paid to do, Grigor tells me, I'm here to work the new computer system and keep Zebadie on track and attend therapy sessions with Grigor when he thinks I need them, so there's some semi−déjà vu for me too.

Boiler suit lady is not even out through the door before Zebadie says, a little too loud, "Didn't you fuck him in the backseat of his Porsche?"

"Who?" I ask. "Which Porsche?"

"Barry."

"Well," I say, my voice low and directed towards the counter top, "it was Grigor's Porsche. But I *thought* it was Barry."

Zebadie's eyes bulge. "But they're not even identical."

"I know. But Grigor and I ... it was a very messy evening and I had a cold and I couldn't smell."

Zebadie shakes her head and smirks, like she's just discovered the Theory of Relativity while I can't even count to ten. She slaps the large appointment book shut, pushes it aside, then reaches for her wedding planner again. It opens on three long fabric swatches, pale purple ribbons stuck to the page with clear sticky tape.

"Lilac, mauve or lavender," Zebadie says. "It's so hard choosing the right colour for my bridesmaids." She pushes the scrapbook in front of me. "What do you think?"

I look at the fabric swatches again, shiny and pale purple and I can't decide which is lilac and which is mauve and which is lavender. I set my face in an interested look: eyebrows raised and eyes wide. "Choose the one that's easiest to spell."

Looking up, I see Grigor poking his head around the door. "Morgana?"

He cups his hand over the receiver but his voice draws me in — tones so even and measured and demanding to be listened to — so I hear every syllable like I'm sitting on his lap.

"I want it perfect for the wedding," he says. "My fiancée is giving it to me for a wedding gift. I want to remove this flaring" — he brushes his nostrils with his free hand — "and I want a more aquiline line. This bump" — now he touches just below the bridge of his nose — "is ruining an otherwise perfect profile."

Actually sitting on the black leather armchair — titanium frame, tight across the seat: elegant but unyielding — I cross my knees and my right ankle starts twitching like a metronome. I read the nameplate on the desk: Grigor Smiroveich™. When we married he was Grigor Smith. Before that he was Greg Smith. Now he's a trademarked Russian.

He drops the receiver back into its cradle and opens the file marked *Morgana Malone* on his desk.

"You know what would be the perfect wedding gift," he says, closing my file again. And as he looks up, his eyes mist over. "Oh, I don't know if I dare."

He looks at his hands on the desk, strokes his nose again, and opens his mouth to speak. Then stops. Is he blushing?

"Your face is red, Grigor."

Grigor coughs. "It's just a bit of pre–surgery swelling," he says. "Marrying a former adult entertainer drives my need to improve my looks."

He opens my file again then snaps it shut.

"You know what would be the perfect wedding gift?" he says again, now looking straight at me.

A penis extension? I want to say.

"Something that will mean just as much to Zebadie as it will to me."

A penis extension? I want to say.

"We'd really like you to be Zebadie's matron of honour on our wedding day."

I think that's the day I'm having my penis extension, I want to say.

"Barry's going to be best man," he adds.

My jaw flaps in mid–air but nothing comes out of my mouth. So it's lucky the 'phone rings and Grigor picks it up.

Zebadie's telephone voice, shrill and nasal and garbled, pierces through the plastic.

"Yes," he says, "she's smiling and looking very pleased." And then he looks over at me. "Lavender, mauve or lilac?" Grigor asks. "Zebadie wants to know."

"Lavender," I say, presuming it's the right answer. But when I picture myself standing at the altar and taking Zebadie's bouquet of wild cherries and spinifex from her re—virginated hand, I can only see myself in pale violet.

Wednesday, 26th February 2014

Dylan, A Love Story

by Gary Percesepe

My ex calls. It's about the dog of the family. Dylan is dying, she explains. There are decisions to make.

I met Savannah when I was nineteen, married at twenty-one. We divorced, after more than thirty years. I'd had an affair. She'd waited till near the end to have hers. In between we'd reared two children in the company of canines.

Dylan is a white standard poodle. If he makes it through the long Ohio winter, he will be fourteen years old in April.

Having seen us through the end of a marriage, Dylan's time is near.

His eyes are dull. His hearing is failing. He falls a lot, and is incontinent. Worse, Savannah says he appears to be in pain, with hip dysplasia, lower back trouble, and a spindly hind leg he can't use.

Shortly after we met, Savannah showed me a picture of Sandy, a cocker spaniel she'd taught to balance on a seesaw. Sandy holds a Lucky Strike cigarette between her teeth.

A newspaper photographer snapped the picture at her grandfather's house, where she'd gone to live after her alcoholic father abandoned her. Maybe her grandfather thought the picture would cheer her up. It was taken just before dark, in the gloaming.

Savannah's mouth is set in a straight line. Her pale blue eyes are fixed on Sandy; she concentrates on staying balanced. The picture was taken shortly after her mother died of cancer, at forty. Savannah was eight.

It is the same expression she had in one of our wedding photos, I later realized.

We met in college. Our courtship was a series of contests, to prove how much I loved her. I passed every test. She called me her knight, come to the rescue. At nineteen, I liked hearing that. I was sure I could make her happy.

But six years into our marriage I had an affair. The marriage survived, but Cupid's arrow had festered, an arrow too deep to be driven through and impossible to pull out. I agonized over things that could not be fixed, and understood that, from some things, there is no rescue. In the last two years of our marriage, she had an affair with a guy from high school she'd reconnected with on Facebook.

When I asked her to marry me, Savannah asked one thing: that I never abandon her. We lasted across four decades. Dylan is the last dog we had together.

On the phone Savannah explains that she can no longer carry Dylan up the long winding staircase to her bedroom, and down again in the early morning, for fear of falling herself.

My new landlord won't allow dogs.

Euthanizing him may the best thing, Savannah thinks. "He was always your dog," she says. "But he's been such a comfort to me here. I really appreciate you letting him stay with me. But since you moved out he's been giving up."

She asks if I want to come see Dylan. I tell her I'll be right over.

I cut the engine, and look at my former home. All fourteen rooms hold holiday candles. An Italianate villa, with emphatic eaves supported by corbels, a low slung roof, and six brick chimneys for Santa to choose from, the house is guarded by an antique wrought iron fence and a tall hedge. The neighborhood is scarred by high poverty and failing schools. We were urban pioneers when we moved here in 1997.

A year after we moved in, I contacted a breeder I admired in San Luis Obispo. I stressed that I wanted a male. She described a white charmer, borderline show quality but perfect as a pet, with an even temperament but plenty of attitude. How much? I asked. A thousand, plus the plane ticket from California. I told her to ship him to Dayton, Ohio as soon as possible.

Dylan took the redeye. He arrived the next morning, pristine, a study in elegance. His coat was gleaming white, with flashing black eyes and nose; his top knot and tail fluffed, he sported a puppy cut that made him look like a lion. His shipping crate was unsoiled. He stood squarely on four big feet and smiled that killer smile, his pink tongue set between razor sharp puppy teeth, his short wiry tail banging against the bars of the crate.

I carried the crate into the kitchen. Grabbing a camera, I sprung him loose. He walked free like a movie star hitting his mark, facing the flashing paparazzi, the tiled kitchen floor his red carpet. He followed me like — well, like a dog. I took one step forward, he took one step forward. I took one step back, he took one step back. I reached down to hug him, pulling him into my chest. His hair smelled of California shampoo, and his nose was wet against my cheek. He was the size of a Miniature Schnauzer, but those big feet promised growth. By his first birthday he would stand twenty four inches at the shoulder and weigh over fifty pounds.

I think about that day often, Dylan in the kitchen. We were inseparable, Peter Pan sewed to his shadow.

Dylan was not our first standard poodle. When I was a graduate student in Saint Louis we purchased a large white male. Amour was on hand to welcome Sammy's birth. Janelle was three. Soon after, I was offered a teaching position at a small liberal arts college. We moved to a twelve acre spread in the Ohio countryside. Off his leash at last, Amour chased our horses, and terrorized the barn cats and peacocks. I walked the property with him, showing him the road and trying to find a common language, the language of no, danger, stop.

One morning I walked toward the road to check the mail. Amour flashed by, a white blur chasing a cat. I screamed, "Stop!" but it was too late. Brakes squealed, then a dull thud. Amour walked away, and I took heart. He staggered to me, then collapsed at my feet, dead. The driver cried apologies, but I waved him off without a word. I carried Amour's broken body to the house, dug a hole, gathered Savannah and the kids. We shared favorite memories, said a prayer.

More pets would die. The road was a cruel presence. We had an Australian Shepherd with bright blue eyes. I found him dead by the door one day, a note attached to his collar. One day a pack of wild dogs savaged our rabbit hutch. Janelle came tearing through the house, screaming, "Dad, quick!" I grabbed my rifle and shot one of the dogs as he lunged at my throat. He fell in a heap, a bullet in his head. The others ran off, but the bunnies were dead.

Jesse was our second standard poodle. Savannah named him after Jesse James, because he was a thief. When one of the kids

117

was missing a stuffed animal or a mate to a sock, we learned to check Jesse's dog run. At dinner one night he walked off with a sixteen-ounce porterhouse steak. Shimmering black, he was a bit undersized, but had personality to spare. He babysat the kids. They'd feed him popcorn by the fireplace, and he helped with their homework, listening to nightly complaints about math.

Jesse got cancer in his thirteenth year. By then, Janelle was in college, Sammy in ninth grade. We assembled again and said goodbye to our thieving friend.

The kids were gone when Dylan came to live with us. He was the first dog Savannah and I had to ourselves. A snowstorm hit just after his first Christmas in Ohio. A newspaper photographer snapped a picture of Dylan leaping and twisting in the air on the snowy street. The next morning, Dylan was splashed across the front page, with the caption, "Blowin' in the Wind."

I sometimes think that Dylan was an ambassador. Everywhere he went he made friends. I am convinced he kept Savannah and I together when our marriage ran out of steam. He was our baby. We stayed together for the sake of the child? Maybe. Or maybe we just loved the way he stayed present with us during days of unbearable loneliness in the house, our love dying as embers in the fireplace. He'd pad up to me and nuzzle his head in my lap, then go to Savannah and do the same, allowing us to transfer to him the affection we still had for each other but were somehow unable to express. Never once did that dog disappoint us. He was a conduit of unconditional love.

Last month I took Dylan to get clipped. Savannah had gone to see her Facebook boyfriend, and I had custody for a month. I had met a woman in New York City who knocked me out. Neither of us is ready for "a relationship." The barriers seem insurmountable. Pari's going through a difficult divorce, I'm considerably older, and we live in different states. We joke about how "it's *so* not us." But having her in my life, however complicated, has been a comfort

Coming out of the clip joint, walking to my open convertible, I tried to explain the situation to Dylan. He listened without judgment, as always. Blow dried and pampered, he sat upright in the passenger seat. He smiled at his parking lot admirers who clustered and pointed, oohed and ahhed. He really was a movie star.

I knock at the back door. Savannah opens it, and lets me in. Dylan comes right up to me and buries his muzzle between my legs. I kneel to the floor and hold on to him. I say my goodbyes. Then I get to my feet and tell Savannah I'm grateful for the care she's given Dylan, and will support her decision. She snaps one last picture of the two of us. I'm wearing a ski hat and sunglasses to hide my tears. Naturally, the picture is taken in the kitchen.

Thursday, 27th February 2014

Waking Up Samford Again

by Nathaniel Tower

Samford wakes up to the sight of a decent—looking woman snoozing at his side. Her face is almost pressed against his and the warm breath rhythmically blowing into his nostrils makes him cringe and smile. It makes him feel like a human, for all the good and bad that comes with such a feeling.

Staring at her, not moving, he tries to recall the evening that led him here. This isn't a routine for Samford. It has been a month since he's had this, at least he thinks, and he has no idea how long it had been before that sexual incident, if ever.

He stares at the woman until he starts to remember something. An involuntary flutter of her eyelids sparks his memory, and his eyes squeeze shut so last night's movie can play in his mind.

"My name is Samford," he had said to the woman at the bar. He had no idea why he was in the bar, or even what the bar was called or if he had come alone or somehow with someone else. But he knew he was sitting at the bar with a woman who looked good enough to talk to — especially with drinks — and maybe even good enough to take home.

The woman's head whipped back in surprise, her drink nearly toppling over. "Your name is *Samford*?"

"What?" he had asked.

She settled back on her stool and fingered the rim of her glass. "Oh, nothing. It's just weird because Samford is an unusual name, but I know I've met a Samford before."

Samford shrugged. "I supposed it is a bit of a rarity. I could always be normal and just go by Sam."

"My name is Sarah." She smiled. He had no idea why either of them were at a bar on a Wednesday night. In the present, he has no idea why she is in his bed on a Thursday morning.

Samford recognized the name, but not in the way his had registered with her. Every woman was named Sarah. Or Sara. Or some other variation. He was sure he had slept with many Sarahs before, but he couldn't remember any specific sexual encounters or any specific women named Sarah. The only woman he could remember at all was that crazy scientist—cloning lady he had run away from a month ago. One day shy of a month, that was. This month—long drought embarrassed him, although he supposed it didn't matter since no one knew. He hadn't found any friends since his strange discovery. His only source of human contact was at the grocery store and the occasional run in with a neighbor at his apartment. Of course, he wasn't exactly sure it was his apartment, but it matched the address on the license in his wallet, and no one had bothered him about living there. He had yet to find any clues about his life in the confines of the small space, but at least it was a place to sleep and a place to bring girls named Sarah.

Samford opens his eyes and looks at Sarah again. The drought is over. The twenty—seventh is apparently his lucky day. He recalls the orgasm and how great it had felt. It almost made him not worry about whether or not he's a real person. He couldn't shake the feeling entirely though. If he's just a clone, was he anything more than a dildo attached to a moving body? Could he impregnate Sarah if he hadn't been the product of pregnancy himself? At least not directly.

Samford is snapped out of his orgasmic recollection by something brushing against his penis. He opens his eyes and sees

Sarah sitting up, her right foot caressing his member, trying to get her toes wrapped around it. He becomes rock hard even though the sight of her feet disgusts him. Her toes are too stubby for her long, slender feet, and he thinks he sees more than one corn. He grimaces, but this only makes his dick harder.

"Do you like that?" she asks.

He lets out a soft moan. He doesn't want to like it, but he can't help it. Perhaps he has been programmed this way. He shakes his head. He refuses to accept that he is just a programmed body.

She wedges the shaft between her toes, and squeezes as if trying to crack a nut. Samford yelps. She giggles.

Sarah releases the vice grip of her toes and crawls up to Samford. "So, what's it like?"

"What's what like?" He hopes she doesn't mean the footjob she's trying to give him. He doesn't want to admit how amazing it felt.

"Having sex with a clone, silly." She smiles and shoves her breasts in his face. "Can you even tell these aren't real?"

"You're a clone?" He cups her breasts with both hands and pushes her body away. The flesh feels real to him, but what does he know.

"Of course I am. Didn't you see the serial number on the inside of my anus?"

He breathes in. His lips curl in disgust and his stomach churns at the imaginary smell of shit and butt sweat. "How would I have seen that?"

"You spent plenty of time down there last night." She plops the breasts in his face again. "So, do they feel real?"

He pushes the breasts away again. "Do all clones have a serial number in their anus?"

"I don't know. I just know that's where mine is. I know all clones have one, unless they are illegals."

"Illegals?"

"Yeah. You know, unauthorized."

He stares at her, trying to make her read his thoughts.

"Do you want to see the serial number again?" she asks. This isn't what he had been thinking at all.

"I have a better idea. Why don't you look at my anus?"

Her eyebrows arch. "You mean you might be a clone?"

"I really don't know."

"Then let's have a look."

He flips over with her help and spreads open his cheeks. He can't tell what she's doing back there, but it feels weird. Not necessarily in a bad way though. His penis hardens against the mattress.

"Do you see anything?"

"Hmmm. I do see a little something."

"What is it?"

She pulls her hands away and his cheeks snap shut.

"Nothing."

"What do you mean nothing? You said you saw something."

"I thought I did, but I guess it wasn't. Look, I have to go. Right now."

He tries to turn over and grab her, but she's on her way out before he can even roll to his side. He watches her cloned ass jiggle its way through the door and down the hallway, and wonders why they didn't tighten that a bit in the cloning process.

Still naked, he stands and grabs Sarah's abandoned purse from the bedside. Opening it, he pulls out a brochure. He gapes at the sight of the familiar text and images. The brochure slips from his hand and flutters to the carpet, just as he collapses to his knees.

Friday, 28th February 2014

The Bite

by Kimberlee Smith

Today is two weeks since my and Dean's second wedding anniversary. Every day since he and my mum Maybell brought our baby Etheline Margaret home from the hospital, Dean's been out in the garden just before dawn and again as dusk draws near with Maggie, as he likes to call her, fused to one hip while he wrangles the watering hose with the opposite hand, making sure to soak the roots and electric–green leaf sprouts on the jacaranda saplings he planted as a Christmas present for me. Our home was one of the last to be sold in the new development. The lawn was bare dirt; the grass laid by the builder had long since scorched, dried up, and blown away. Dean set quick smart to rolling out new sod and planting the jacaranda.

The sun is climbing; the sky is a mix of pink and blue fairy floss. Dean forces the trigger on the hose down with such a tight grasp it's like he's shooting a gun. He sprays too hard. The jacarandas tremble. Leaves that haven't had a chance to fully develop flutter off their boughs like butterflies with busted wings. His eyes are red from smoke, liquor, and sleeplessness.

He throws the hose to the ground and, with his free hand, grabs up a fistful of fallen leaves, and aims to toss them into the ravine behind the house. They fall softly, spinning through the air, and some whorl right into his face even though the air is still as a soldier.

And the whole time he cries. Rumbling with stifled tears. The baby is soothed by the rhythmic motion of his gulping breath and becomes drowsy as he rocks toe to heel, like a hobbyhorse. He is trying real hard to hold his shit together.

He and my mum take turns keeping the baby in their rooms, alternating nightly, so they are able to each catch up on lost sleep. Neither one of them suspected they'd end up sharing the mothering duties, and they were ill—prepared. Dean figured I'd do it, and certainly Mum would lend a hand, but not doing it full time at her age. She's only 48 but those 48 years have been long, hard ones.

When it is Dean's night to take care of the baby, as it was last night, he gives in to exhaustion and lets her suck away on a bottle of formula until she's sucking on nothing but air. He tosses and turns; sleep doesn't come easy to him these days. He's become a worrier.

Maggie fusses because she's got a belly overfull of formula and air. He pops a dummy in her mouth and she sucks like heck until that poor little angel chucks up the curdled formula. When will he learn it's worth the time it takes to burp her? The book I bought him on being an expectant father collected dust in the magazine rack whenever he went in the loo to take a crap.

I have the perverse pleasure of watching him sit on the toilet and speed read what he should have been learning all along. Sometimes my husband can be a real fool. You should know that I'm gone. Never had a chance to hold my baby, never got to meet her. It's not that I'm being blameful – but fact of the matter is, it *was* Dean's fault.

The bite. It came just a couple weeks before the baby was due. Hottest summer any of us could recall, but it was the first one I lived anywhere with air conditioning. Not the kind that blows all through the house in vents, but the kind that mounts in a window: an electric box that plugs in to keep one particular room cool. Dean bought them for every room except the spare bedroom where he keeps his snakes. He's an exotic reptile dealer and having the snakes living *with* us was a new arrangement since we moved from the Bonnie Doon Mobile Estate Park down on the chapped lips of Lake Eildon in Victoria, which if you ask me is pretty much the intersection of Absolutely Nowhere and Oh, Well. We made the big move to be closer to Kingsford Smith Airport in Sydney, where all of the stock was moved in to and out from.

I didn't mind his business when he kept it out of the house and his partner, Junior Volpe, kept the snakes at some storage facility in Eastern Creek. They took turns tending to their investment, but when Dean starting bringing in big cash by brokering the deals – being the brains behind the business – Junior put the pressure on Dean to take some of the load off him. Junior's in his late 50s and doesn't have the same energy he used to when he and Dean's daddy were in business together. Fair enough.

Dean bought the house – paid for it outright, in cash – and decorated it without any help. You can tell. There's a black leather sectional sofa with two recliner chairs built–in; it's roomy enough to seat eight people. But we never had so many people in our home at once and I imagine they *never* will. He bought the sofa just because he could. Swallows up the whole damn room, just about. And it's the biggest lounge room I've ever been in.

He bought two waterbeds, one for him and me and one for Maybell, and satin sheets to go with. He has room for a couple dozen terrariums to keep his stock, which includes Taipans, Death Adders, good old American Rattlers, etc, etc, depending. Understanding the laws of supply and demand, you see.

Dean even has room to grow their food. Little white mice. Hundreds of them. Those, he keeps them in the garage in the same kind of glass boxes he keeps the snakes in. You'd think there's no business for snake dealers in Australia, as a continent we have a plentiful supply of dangerous wildlife, but Aussies like to keep exotic snakes not found here; overseas, they like the badass reputation of the snakes that are native to our country.

Every buyer wants what's hard to get. Human nature. The craziest part of the business is the exporting. The guys who do that for a living, working under Dean and Junior, risk their lives every time they transport those snakes on flights that are at least half a day or night long. Ironically not one of the smugglers has been fatally bitten yet. I'm the one who succumbed to death by snakebite because I cohabitated with them. In a very short while we got used to them being around all the time. That was the big mistake.

That singular day, the sun stretched over the Blue Mountains, casting shadows the color of tobacco spit on the houses in our development. The asphalt streets were so hot they turned spongy and soft, sticking to children's bicycle wheels like chewing gum, causing them to flip and fall over while the neighbourhood dogs furiously licked the tar that burned the pads of their paws.

There was a colossal dust storm on the M4 where an 18−wheel truck jackknifed and closed the motorway down in both directions for two days. Bushfires ripped across the Southern Highlands and charred every type of animal life: sulphur−crested cockatoos and rainbow−hued lorikeets fell from the skies, wings singed. Wombats perished from smoke inhalation as they hunkered deeper down into their burrows. Eucalyptus trees became burning bushes baring skeletons of koalas, with babies never having a chance to peer outside their mums' pouches. Only the platypuses survived unscathed, but of course they're cranky and sneaky as all get out, so when their bogs were invaded by immolating creatures they were miserable beyond usual. Armageddon seemed to be upon us all.

It was my third trimester of pregnancy. I grew heavy and swollen. It was impossible for me to lower myself down on the waterbed mattress that wiggled like jelly and forget about those slippery satin sheets. No matter how concerted my efforts, every time I lowered myself onto the bed I sunk so deep my tailbone smacked the base. Whenever I tried to roll out of the bed, I'd get a stitch in my side. I was peeing a bunch of times every night so it became exercise too rigorous. As newlyweds we whispered often about how fun it would be to roll around on a waterbed. Of course that was until we owned one. Like many experiences you don't realize are overrated until you have them, sleeping on a waterbed ranks right up there.

In the last few weeks of my life, I took to sleeping downstairs on the leather sectional sofa that was nice and stiff. If Dean hadn't bought waterbeds, or a new house big enough to keep those snakes – especially the pair of Coral snakes that he had to hold onto a few extra days longer than usual for a client who was tending to business in Southeast Asia (I don't ever ask what kind of business his customers are tied into) and kept a dominatrix den next to his wine cellar – then I would still be there today with him, raising our daughter with the beautiful name we chose together. Mum picked Etheline. Dean was in shock and could not protest. He's wrong about being alone now; I'm there with him. He just doesn't have the sensitivity to my presence.

§

This morning Maybell is taking Etheline Margaret for a stroll in her pram around the neighborhood before it gets too hot for them to leave the house. Even though there's a shade attachment to the pram, little Etheline's eyes are watery slits. Today I notice they've changed from the grayish—blue color many fair—skinned babies are born with to deep amber, like a rich lager. I'm trying not to think about how serpent—like they are, yet they're the most beautiful eyes I've ever seen.

Maybell notices. Dean notices. They don't say a word about it. Dean is spending hours threading together twenty rattles from the snakes he traded, captured, bought and sold. These particular ones are Sidewinders, Western Diamondbacks, and Baja rattlers imported from North America. It's all he can think to do to make something good out of something so bad.

Back to the day of the bite, the extreme heat caused the earth below us to move. Tectonic plates expanded, shifted, and quaked. The temblor that hit us was only a 1.6 magnitude on the Richter scale, but it was enough to knock out the electrical power for a couple hours. We were all dead asleep, but the snakes felt it coming well before the earthquake hit. Their terrariums were stacked up on snap—together plastic shelving Dean put together himself, and he might have done a better job of it. I stumbled down the hall to the loo, bracing myself against the walls from the lounge where I slept, through the kitchen, and then approached the reptile den on my way to pee. The air was dark as squid ink and if I had tried to see my hand in front of my face, I would have smacked myself in the nose.

That's when I felt a rolling squish under my foot and right after a fierce plunge of razor—sharp fangs into the meat of my calf. It was so clean it didn't hurt at first, but then the snake dug in again and again. Then the pain stole my breath. I fell to the floor and tried to scream, but I could not get one sound out. The whole episode lasted about five minutes, I reckon. Then that was it.

The thud of my body against the floor is what must've woken Dean. The power flickered back on and I watched him – from right above his shoulders – race down the staircase to find me splayed out like a busted doll, snakes writhing all around. I saw it all like I was watching a movie. I was gone.

Etheline Margaret took a long afternoon nap while Dean finished up making her rattle toy. Maybell is back in the kitchen putting frozen meat pies in the oven for tea and is drinking lemon squash with a splash of gin. Her fifth of the day. Dean has sweet Maggie in his arms and they lock eyes. He knows there's serpent in her now. She looks at him so wisely, like she's a thousand years old. And I believe she is. He takes the rattle and slides it over her plump little fist and before he can blink she slips one of those nubbed spires – one from a Sidewinder – between her lips, suckles on it, and smiles up at him.

Authors

Rachel Ambrose is a twenty–something fiction writer from Connecticut. Her favorite season is winter, she enjoys well–made Manhattans, and she loves Southern fiction. Her work has appeared in *Crack the Spine*, *Exiles Literary Magazine*, and *The Colton Review*. She is currently at work on her second novel and blogs at http://victorywhiskeyjuliet.tumblr.com.

Lynn Beighley is a fiction writer stuck in a technical book writer's body. Her stories often involve deeply flawed characters and the unsatisfying meshing of the virtual and actual world. She has an MFA in Creative Writing and currently has 16 books published.

Margaret Bingel is just a writer, living in Manchester, New Hampshire. She spends her time working at her father's beer store, art modeling, and writing (when she can). She doesn't have a website or a blog yet, but who knows, maybe she'll have one in the future.

Guilie Castillo–Oriard is a Mexican writer currently exiled in the island of Curaçao. She misses Mexican food and Mexican *amabilidad*, but the laissez–faire attitude and the beaches of the Caribbean are fair exchange. Plus, the bounty of cultural diversity inspires great culture–clash fiction. Guilie is currently revising and editing her first novel. Her short stories have appeared in *Fiction 365*, *Lady Ink Magazine* and *Pure Slush*. She blogs at http://guilie–castillo–oriard.blogspot.com.

John Wentworth Chapin lives and writes in Baltimore, where he is too frequently starting Project B before finishing Project A. John writes non–fiction as well as fiction. Find him on the web at http://johnwentworthchapin.com.

James Claffey hails from County Westmeath, Ireland, and lives on an avocado ranch in Carpinteria, CA with his family. He is the author of a collection of short fiction, *Blood a Cold Blue*. His website can be found at http://jamesclaffey.com.

Gay Degani has published online and in print including *The Best of Every Day Fiction* editions and her own collection, *Pomegranate Stories*. She is the founder–editor emeritus of EDF's *Flash Fiction Chronicles*, a staff editor at *Smokelong Quarterly*, and blogs at http://wordsinplace.blogspot.com where a list of her work can be found. She's had two stories nominated for Pushcart consideration and won the eleventh Annual Glass Woman Prize for her flash piece, *Something about L.A..*.

Michelle Elvy is an editor and writer who has meandered from the shores of the Chesapeake to New Zealand's Bay of Islands. Michelle has published poetry, short stories and non–fiction about travel, faraway places, food, motorcycling, slow travel, the kindness of strangers and raising children in unusual places for numerous literary journals and magazines in the US, Canada, Australasia, the UK and Europe. She edits at *Flash Frontier: An Adventure in Short Fiction* and *Blue Five Notebook*. She can also be found regularly at *Awkword Paper Cut*. More about manuscript assessment and Michelle's take on editing and writing can be found at http://michelleelvy.com.

Gloria Garfunkel is the daughter of two Auschwitz survivors which deeply affected her whole life and personality. She has a Ph.D. from Harvard University in Psychology and Social Relations, concentrating on Personality Development Studies. She was a psychotherapist for thirty years working with children, adults and families. She is currently retired, reading and writing to her heart's content. She has published many stories in journals and anthologies and hopes to eventually publish a collection of her flash fiction. You can find more of her work at her blog http://queruloussquirreldaily.blogspot.com/.

Teresa Burns Gunther has had fiction and non–fiction appear in numerous literary journals and most recently in *Northwind Magazine, Bookslut* and *Best New Writing 2012*. Teresa is the Editor of *The Lakeside*, an online literary magazine, and she founded Lakeshore Writers Workshop in Oakland, California where she leads creative writing workshops and classes and works one–on–one with writers. You can find links to her work at http://www.teresaburnsgunther.com/.

Gill Hoffs lives with her family and an ever–dwindling supply of Nutella in the North of England. Find Gill on Facebook or as @gillhoffs on twitter, email her a dirty joke at gillhoffs@hotmail.co.uk, or leave a clean comment at http://gillhoffs.wordpress.com/. *Wild: a collection* was published by *Pure Slush Books* in 2012. Her non–fiction book *The Sinking of RMS Tayleur: the Lost Story of the Victorian Titanic* is out now from *Pen & Sword*. Feel free to send her chocolate.

Len Kuntz is a writer from Washington State and an editor at the online literary magazine *Metazen*. His work appears widely in print and online. Find him at http://lenkuntz.blogspot.com.

Sally–Anne Macomber was born and raised in Toronto, Canada, and studied journalism at Concordia University in

Montreal. Her work on high fashion and the demise of haute couture has appeared in various online and print publications in both Europe and North America. She turned to writing flash fiction in 2010, and hasn't looked back.

Jessica McHugh is an author of speculative fiction that spans the genre from horror and alternate history to epic fantasy. A member of the Horror Writers Association and a 2013 Pulp Ark nominee, she has devoted herself to novels, short stories, poetry, and playwriting. Jessica has had thirteen books published in five years, including the bestselling *Rabbits in the Garden*, *The Sky: The World* and the gritty coming–of–age thriller, *PINS*. More info on her speculations and publications can be found at http://www.jessicamchughbooks.com.

Gwendolyn Joyce Mintz is a fiction writer and aspiring photographer. Her work has appeared in various online and print publications. In other incarnations, Mintz is a writing instructor, a teddy bear maker and somebody's grandmother.

Mandy Nicol grew up in Melbourne, Australia and made a tree change to country Victoria in the mid–nineties – the decade, not her age. She has various animals including a flockette of pet sheep that are thankful for her vegaquarian habits. She writes short stories and loves flash fiction. *Pure Slush* is the first venue to publish her work.

Derek Osborne lives in eastern Pennsylvania. His work has appeared in *Boston Literary Magazine*, *Bartleby Snopes*, *Literary Orphans*, *The Linnet's Wings*, *Pure Slush* and many others. To read more visit http://gertrudesflat.blogspot.com, or email him at derekosborne1@gmail.com.

Gary Percesepe is Associate Editor at *New World Writing* (formerly *Mississippi Review*) and a Contributor at *The Nervous*

Breakdown. Author of four books in philosophy, Percesepe's poetry, fiction, essays, and interviews have appeared in *Story Quarterly*, *N + 1*, *Salon*, *Mississippi Review*, *The Millions*, *Brevity*, *PANK*, *Metazen*, *The Brooklyner*, and other places. His collection of short stories, *Why I Did the Grocery Girl*, is forthcoming from Aqueous Books. His poetry collection *falling* and his flash fiction collection *itch* were published by *Pure Slush Books* in late 2013. He has taught at Saint Louis University, Wittenberg University, and University of Dayton. He lives in Buffalo, New York.

Matt Potter is an Australian–born writer who keeps a part of his psyche in Berlin. Matt has been published in various places online, and he is, rather amazingly, also the founding editor of *Pure Slush*. You can find more of his work at his website: http://mattcpotter.webs.com/.

Darryl Price was born in Kentucky and educated at Thomas More College. A founding member of L. Jack Roth's Yellow Pages Poets, he has published dozens of chapbooks, and his poems have appeared in many journals. He currently edits *Olentangy Review* with his wife Melissa.

Stephen V. Ramey is an American author from New Castle, Pennsylvania. His work has appeared in many places, including *The Doctor TJ Eckleburg Review*, *The Journal of Compressed Creative Arts*, and *A Capella Zoo*. *Glass Animals*, his first collection of (very) short fiction is available from *Pure Slush Books*. Find him and more of his work at his website: http://www.stephenvramey.com.

Shane Simmons is a self–confessed coffee shop writer who believes that regardless of quality, each paragraph penned should be rewarded with sweet treats (cake, muffins, Belgian waffles, etc). London–born, he ran away to Glasgow ten years ago. Since then he has expanded his waistline and he now blogs at http://scribblingsimmons.wordpress.com/.

Kimberlee Smith is a writer whose poetry, essays, fiction, and creative non–fiction have been published in numerous literary journals and anthologies. She was awarded a residency to the Jentel Arts Program in 2013. She lives with her two daughters, two dogs, three cats, two rabbits, and nine chooks on her farm in rural Connecticut. She received her MA in English from the University of Sydney, a certificate in the Creative Writing Program through UCLA, and her BA in Journalism from the University of Southern California. She is enrolled currently in post–graduate studies at Columbia University in New York. She can do a headstand on a trampoline, kill a chook, and make hard cider from the apples in her orchard.

Andrew Stancek was born in Bratislava and saw Russian tanks occupying his homeland. His dreams of circuses and ice cream, flying and lion–taming, miracle and romance have appeared recently in print in *LA Review*, *Windsor Review* and *New Sun Rising: Stories for Japan*. Among the many online publications featuring his work are *Every Day Fiction*, *Gemini Magazine* (Flash Fiction Contest Grand Prize Winner), *fwriction*, *r.kv.r.y. quarterly literary journal*, *Tin House*, *Flash Fiction Chronicles*, *The Linnet's Wings*, *Connotation Press*, *THIS Literary Magazine*, *LA Review*, *Windsor Review*, *Thrice Fiction Magazine*, *New Sun Rising*, and *Pure Slush*.

Susan Tepper is the author of four published books of fiction and a chapbook of poetry. Her most recent title *The Merrill Diaries* (*Pure Slush Books*, July 2013) is a Novel in Stories that follow a young woman's adventures in love and lust on two continents, spanning a decade. Tepper has received nine Pushcart nominations, and one for the Pulitzer Prize in fiction. You can visit her website here: http://www.susantepper.com.

Nathaniel Tower lives in the Twin Cities with his wife and daughter. After teaching high school English for nine years, he decided to pursue a career in writing / publishing / editing. His fiction has appeared in over two hundred online and print journals. His first collection of fiction, *Nagging Wives, Foolish Husbands*, was released in 2013 through *Martian Lit*. Nathaniel is the founding and managing editor of *Bartleby Snopes Literary Magazine and Press*. Find out more about Nathaniel at http://nathanieltower.wordpress.com.

Townsend Walker lives in San Francisco. His stories have been published in over fifty literary journals and included in seven anthologies. One story won the SLO NightWriters story contest. Two were nominated for the PEN / O. Henry Award. Four were performed at the New Short Fiction Series in Hollywood. He is associate editor at *Grey Sparrow Journal*. During a career in finance he published three books, on foreign exchange, derivatives and portfolio management. Educated at Georgetown, NYU and Stanford, you can find his website at http://www.townsendwalker.com.

Michael Webb is continually surprised anyone is interested in what he has to say, and he blogs occasionally at http://innocentsaccidentshints.blogspot.com.

Other anthologies from Pure Slush
Visit the Pure Slush Store:
http://pureslush.webs.com/store.htm

January 2014 Vol. 1
ISBN: 978−1−925101−03−4

March 2014 Vol. 3
ISBN: 978−1−925101−17−1

April 2014 Vol. 4
ISBN: 978−1−925101−27−0

May 2014 Vol. 5
ISBN: 978−1−925101−30−0

barcode
Pure Slush Vol. 8
ISBN: 978−1−925101−00−3
There's something wonderfully sleazy — and levelling — about bars and bar stories. They certainly don't *have* to be sleazy but there's always the possibility that a bit of alcohol and some smoking and hair let down and belts loosened can lead to candour and laughter and exposé.

Don't glug these stories down all in a single session: give each one the savouring and the contemplation it deserves. Too much, too soon? No one likes a sloppy drunk! Now, who's buying the next round?   *Originally published August 2013*

Catherine refracted
Pure Slush Vol. 7
ISBN: 978−1−304−12272−8
Legands abound about Catherine the Great, Empress and Autocrat of All the Russias.

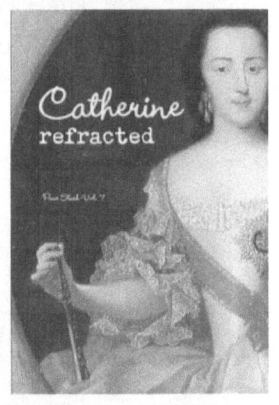

Catherine refracted is a re−imagining of the life and the legends of Catherine the Great. Her lovers, her illegitimate children, her wiles, her wit and her place in history ... all feature in this lively reinterpretation of one of history's most beloved and reviled leaders. Featuring the work of nineteen writers, including rare juvenilia and modern reappraisals of Catherine the Great's place in world cultural history.

Originally published June 2013

obit. Pure Slush Vol. 6

ISBN: 978-1-300-86001-3
Webster Murphy Allen 1925 – 2012. Lawyer, opera-goer, philanthropist, father, grandfather, generous with his time and talents and money ... or was he?

obit. explores the many sides of a man many people *thought* they knew. Each writer has taken an incident or anecdote or memory from Webster's life and created a fully-fleshed man with multiple quirks ... and maybe even multiple secrets. Where does the truth lie?

Featuring thirty-two different stories by twenty-two different writers. *Originally published March 2013*

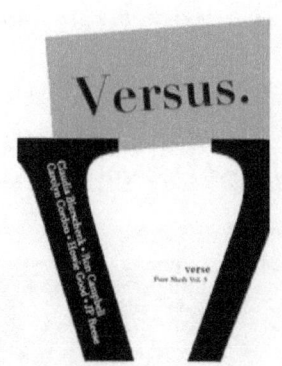

Versus. Pure Slush Vol. 5

ISBN: 978-1-300-76169-3
Can good poetry be written on demand? The answer is "Yes" and *Versus.* is the proof.

Bill Yarrow

5 poets write 15 poems each against 15 different topics – drink, seasons, convenience stores, marriage, chores, personal grooming, budgets, interior decoration, gender, public transport, church, raising children, politics, guilty pleasures, future – so the collection features 75 different opinions. All are different and unique in their own way.

Originally published February 2013

gorge

Pure Slush Vol. 4

a novel in stories

gorge: a novel in stories
Pure Slush Vol. 4
ISBN: 978−1−300−54979−6
Fifty−four stories told by thirty−three writers. Each story is a chapter in the tale of the misplaced Café Gano, a restaurant in a small town on the Maine coast.

The action takes place over one day, and as the afternoon progresses and the evening unfolds, customers' lives unravel and staff decorum snaps to erupt in a crescendo of miscalculated faith and desperate bids for ultimate control. Yeah, it's that crazy!!

For any person who has ever worked in a restaurant, or been a patron, you will laugh aloud at the follies, wonder who will hook up with whom, and at the pace I read this, ask yourself, when will *Pure Slush* bring out the next novel of compilations?
Robert Vaughan

Recommended, particularly if you appreciate a bold experiment in narrative and variety of perspective.   *Stephen V. Ramey*
Originally published December 2012

real Pure Slush Vol. 3
ISBN: 978−1−291−14109−2
upfront! uptight! up−yours! Cutting edge non−fiction from thirty−one writers who spill their guts on life and love, sex and travel, food and legalities and freedom and family, reflecting the true diversity of everyday experience.
Originally published October 2012

real
Pure Slush Vol. 3

Notausgang: emergency exit
Pure Slush Vol. 2
ISBN: 978−1−4717−0059−0
Stories desperate and amusing, based on the theme *emergency exit*. Scary, creepy, funny, illuminating, sad and life−affirming. Twenty−four stories, fiction and non−fiction.

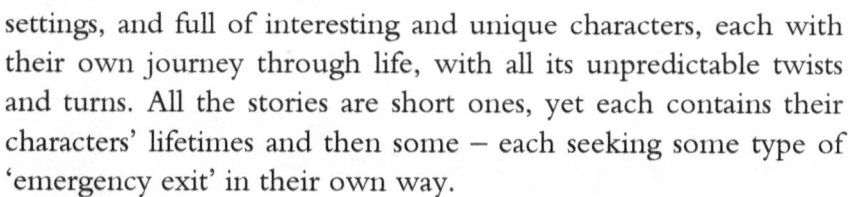

Every story in this collection, while based on the same theme, is well−crafted, rich in the detail of countless settings, and full of interesting and unique characters, each with their own journey through life, with all its unpredictable twists and turns. All the stories are short ones, yet each contains their characters' lifetimes and then some − each seeking some type of 'emergency exit' in their own way.
Joyce Juzwik

Originally published May 2012

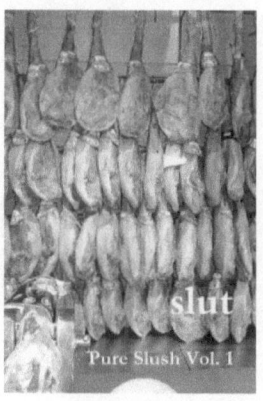

slut Pure Slush Vol. 1
(2nd edition)
ISBN: 978−1−4716−0674−8
a zesty, amusing (and serious) anthology of fiction and non−fiction on the theme 'slut' ... where it all began!!

Originally published February 2012

For the complete range of Pure Slush print books and eBooks, visit the Pure Slush Store at http://pureslush.webs.com/store.htm.

www.ingramcontent.com/pod-product-compliance
Lightning Source LLC
Chambersburg PA
CBHW050822180626
46814CB00004B/1423